REVENGE WITHOUT REMORSE

Alex Salaiz

FriesenPress

Suite 300 - 990 Fort St
Victoria, BC, V8V 3K2
Canada

www.friesenpress.com

First Edition — 2018

ISBN
978-1-5255-2748-7 (Hardcover)
978-1-5255-2749-4 (Paperback)
978-1-5255-2750-0 (eBook)

1. FICTION, THRILLERS, TERRORISM

Distributed to the trade by The Ingram Book Company

Chapter 1

Toronto, Canada

The terrorist agent, an ISIS sleeper residing in Toronto, was still in bed, even though it was going on one in the afternoon. It was a cold day in the provincial capital of Ontario, with light freezing rain falling, making it a perfect day for doing nothing but being lazy and staying in bed. He got up, made a cup of his favorite Arabica coffee, turned the radio on to a soft music station, and then went back to bed. He had called in sick earlier in the morning and given his supervisor a lame excuse, one that his idiot supervisor accepted without question. Stupid ass. He started reading the encrypted email he'd received on his small but very reliable laptop from the Middle Eastern terrorist Abu al-Baghdadi, leader of the Islamic State in Iraq and Syria, directing him to perform an important "martyr duty" in support of all Islamic believers. Despite the Russian claim and rumors flying around that al-Baghdadi had been killed in May 2017 in a raid outside Raqqa, the ISIS de facto capital in Syria, he was very much alive and still very active in directing the everyday operations of the ISIS terror group.

Niko knew exactly what the ISIS leader meant when he used the words "martyr duty"; he didn't have to read between the lines, above the lines, or below the lines. He knew very well what al-Baghdadi meant by martyr duty because he knew him personally, having met him the first time he traveled to fight against the crusaders in Syria as a holy warrior of the caliphate, and had stayed in touch with him since then. Niko had become a Canadian citizen more than twenty years ago but had traveled to Syria and Iraq on two different occasions during that time to fight for the Muslim cause.

Niko Adel Kadyrov was a thirty-eight-year-old bachelor from Tashkent, the capital of Uzbekistan, a former state of the Soviet Union but now a free and independent country since 1991. He had emigrated from Uzbekistan but was born in Chechnya before his parents moved to Uzbekistan when he was two years old. Chechnya was another former Soviet Union state presently free from Putin's authoritarian rule. Niko was well-known and very popular among his Canadian friends for his gregarious manner and unique Cheshire cat grin. He was living comfortably in the city once known as Hogtown and was making a very good living employed as a website builder specializing in advanced website designs and encoding tools.

Now Niko was facing a troubling personal dilemma with his continuously diminishing religious beliefs. He had been introduced by his Western friends in Toronto to other forms of religious dogma, but Niko had kept practicing his Islamic faith though he no longer felt an inner desire to continue with it. To put it bluntly, he did not fully believe in it anymore. He was doubting his religious convictions, even though he came from the Muslim city of Tashkent, a city that claims to have the oldest Koran in the world, the Uthman Koran, inscribed by hand on calfskin and still in flawless condition. Niko had been raised as a Sunni Muslim. The problem was, he'd been exposed to forbidden Western ideas and customs, which he fully enjoyed, but which were considered sins by his religious leaders. Regardless, Niko appreciated and freely participated, without reservation, in the various Western customs he'd been exposed to during the past twenty-plus years he'd lived in Canada. He really enjoyed the Western life, especially the nightlife, frequently visiting numerous gentlemen's nightclubs where beautiful, scantily dressed ladies danced for his enjoyment. Niko was not willing to give all of this up and simply walk away from it. No way, baby.

He couldn't find it in his heart or in his conscience to do what al-Baghdadi was asking him to do. Maybe he could do it but not carry out the mission as a "martyr duty" obligation. He knew he would be compensated very well in American dollars for carrying out the Daesh leader's request. Niko had no problem with the money. The problem was that the ISIS terror group leader would give him a large sum of money and then expect him to die while carrying out the mission. Niko knew for a fact he wouldn't be able to enjoy spending the money once he was dead. That was a no-brainer. No, martyring himself did not make any sense to him. He decided he would carry out the dictates of the ISIS leader, but he'd be damned if he was going to die in the process. Life was too good and sweet in the West to give it up and simply walk away. No, he was not quite ready to die for a Muslim cause, or any other cause, for that matter. Not yet, or maybe never. Niko decided to read the email slowly and deliberately and see if he could find a way to accomplish the holy mission and still live.

"Destroy the infidel's soul and will by executing all of his family members. This will teach the infidel that we will not tolerate his interference with our Muslim goals and missions."

But it was more than just interfering with their Muslim goals and missions. The United States, referred to by the ISIS leaders as the Satan nation, had elected a new president, with the help of Russia, and he had been quoted during the presidential campaign as saying that he would "take out the families" of all of the terrorists that waged war against his country. Well, Niko decided he would deliver a message to the new president and to the rest of the infidel nations. The Muslim people would not take it anymore without appropriate action, especially after a recent bombing raid that killed more than one hundred innocent civilians during a prayer service in Idlib, a small village in Syria. He figured his actions would be payback for the bombings conducted by the American military central command carrying out the campaign promise of the new Republican president. This was the second attack in Syria against the poor and innocent Muslim population since this president had taken office. Enough was enough.

Niko returned his thoughts to the email. He knew who the infidel was the terrorist Daesh leader was referring to. He was the infamous FBI Special Agent Chad Winters, the alleged big thorn on the side of al-Qaeda, Jaish-e-Mohammed, and ISIS leaders.

Unbeknownst to Niko, his email from al-Baghdadi had been intercepted and read as he decrypted the message. The interceptor of the email had been tracking Niko for the past couple of years and he was right here in his backyard, in Toronto, real close to him.

Niko was re-reading the email when his friendship with Yusuf Khalifa, known in the United States before his death as Samuel (Sami) Waters, the hot dog vendor, flashed in his mind. He had got to know Yusuf before his friend immigrated to the United States through Canada. He provided Yusuf refuge in a safe house in Toronto on his arrival there from Egypt. Yusuf stayed in the safe house for a short time, waiting for Niko's contact to provide him with a fake American passport with the name of Samuel Waters. And then what happened to brother Sami in the infidel nation after he got his fake passport and illegally relocated there? Well, he had his head blown off by an FBI agent. Before the infidel got the shot off, the news network reported that Sami tried to make a run to save his ass, but his broken leg made it impossible for him to escape. Was Sami a martyr? Niko didn't think so, but it's what people want to believe that makes it real for them.

Truth and untruth compete at the same playing level, mainly because of social media. And that's the problem. What you want to believe as truth is up to you. Most importantly, if it's convenient for you, then it must be true. So, is Sami now limping around in paradise, headless but holding hands with some of the seventy-two dark-eyed beautiful young virgins he was promised? Well, Niko knew now that it was whatever you wanted to believe that made it true for you. He continued to ponder the email message without considering its consequences for his future actions. Consequences were not even in the picture while he contemplated the message. It never entered Niko's mind that once he carried out al-Baghdadi's request, FBI Special Agent Winters would come after him, seeking revenge without any hint of remorse. Niko might be lucky enough to evade the person tracking him through his computer, but he would not be lucky enough to evade the merciless FBI Special Agent Chadwick Winters. The nightmare for Niko Adel Kadyrov was about to begin as soon as he carried out his holy mission.

Chapter 2

It had been more than a year since Special Agent Winters located the nuclear device that Sami smuggled into the United States. Smuggling the nuclear device had been the brainchild of Dr. Ayman al-Zawahiri, the al-Qaeda leader. This was just one of the many schemes al-Zawahiri had come up with to eliminate Winters, but to no avail. Chad found the nuclear device in time and dropped it deep into the Atlantic Ocean, where it detonated without causing major damage or loss of life. He was back on duty and still creating problems for the Middle East terrorist leaders.

The United States had a new leader now and more animosity had been generated among the Muslim population in the Middle East by the executive orders signed by the new president. The president had banned all refugees from seven Muslim nations but a federal US court had ruled against him. The action by the president had driven up anger against the United States throughout the Middle East, especially among the citizens of the seven Muslim nations identified in the president's first executive order.

To soothe some of that anger in the Muslim nations, Niko was going to check where the FBI special agent's family was located, find the family members, and carry out the terrorist leader's mandate. He decided that, if the family had a dog, he was going to eliminate the mongrel as well. Once the mission was completed, the ISIS terror group would take credit and claim it was necessary to counteract the president's racist executive order. Niko was going to recommend that his successful mission be publicized extensively throughout the Middle

East by the Aamaq News Agency to validate it. But he would have to be careful while carrying out the mission and not martyr himself. No, he was not ready to die, but it was time to find the family of the infidel Winters and execute the holy mission. First, he was going to pray to Allah for success, even though his religious beliefs were currently not very strong and diminishing day by day.

A few days later, Niko received another email, but this one was from an alleged al-Baghdadi associate. The associate advised him that his bank account had been credited with a substantial amount of money to cover his expenses in carrying out his mission. Niko knew that most of the deposited funds had been contributed by a large number of sheiks from Qatar but the money trail would go through different channels, usually shell companies, and various banks in different countries to hide the source of the funds. The associate ordered him to proceed with his mission as soon as possible, but Niko knew the order to proceed was coming directly from al-Baghdadi himself. He had personally met al-Baghdadi during his two sixty-day visits to Syria to fight as a soldier of the caliphate and had stayed in contact with the ISIS leader since then, so he knew how al-Baghdadi thought and operated. He'd got to know him very well during those two visits; therefore, he didn't question the authenticity of the request.

Niko flew from Toronto to Dulles International Airport the following week after clearing some web design projects at work with his immediate supervisor. He requested and was approved for forty-five days of leave for a personal emergency, though he didn't tell his supervisor what that emergency was. Once he arrived at Dulles, Niko was questioned at length by a US immigration agent at the international entry point in the airport. His surname, as shown on his Canadian passport, was the same as the present leader of the Chechen Republic, a Putin puppet. Niko would not admit to the fact that he was a cousin of Ramzan Kadyrov, known as the Putin of Chechnya. After an almost hour-long questioning session by a Department of Homeland Security supervisor, he was allowed into the United States. Niko rented a car at the airport and then checked into the nearby Hilton Airport.

Early the next day, he decided to start checking on the infidel's family members there in Washington, D.C., Chad's city of birth. He gathered the information by researching the public records using the computers located in the public library. But he ran into a problem after an extensive two-week research effort trying to find Agent Winters' immediate family members. Winters had no family, as far as he could tell. He'd done a lot of research and come up empty-handed. Niko learned that Winters' mother had passed away and shortly after her death, he lost his father while he was still in the military. There were no other Winters family members in Washington, D.C., that he could tell. But, being stubborn, Niko didn't give up. He couldn't give up. He had a very important mission to complete. Niko went all the way back in his research to when Winters was a young man growing up in Washington, D.C., to see if he could find any extended family members—cousins, uncles, nieces, aunts, any relative living somewhere else. Nothing.

He found out that Winters got a congressional appointment to West Point, received his army commission, and then reported to Fort Hood, Texas, for his first assignment. Niko found an archived news article from the *Killeen Daily Herald* referring to the pending marriage of young Captain Chad Winters to a Ms. Nora Knight, a registered nurse. But the article said the marriage never took place because Nora Knight was shot and killed before the wedding date during a shooting by a deranged individual in the waiting room of the Fort Hood Darnall Army Community Hospital, where she was employed as a civilian registered nurse. Nora Knight had been one of six individuals killed during the shooting rampage. The article had the names of both the groom's and bride's parents. Niko knew from earlier research that Chad's parents were both deceased. But what about the Knights? The Knights would have been Chad's in-laws if Chad and Nora had married. According to the article, Mr. Knight was a retired army sergeant major and Mrs. Knight was a homemaker. That would do for relatives, thought Niko. But were they still living? If they were still alive, both had to be in their late eighties or early nineties. Well, Niko decided he had to find out if they were alive. They would do for family.

He scheduled a flight for the following day from Dulles International Airport to Austin-Bergstrom International Airport in Austin, Texas. From Austin, he would travel to Killeen, Texas, and then it was a short drive from there to continue on his holy mission. According to his research, the Knights were still residing in a small community just outside Killeen. If at least one of them was living, that would do for a relative; he would take one or both out and his mission would be complete, *insha Allah* (God willing).

Chapter 3

Niko got on a direct American Airlines flight from Dulles International to Austin, Texas, arriving at the state capital at three in the afternoon. He rented a car from Hertz at the airport and, after getting directions from the car rental desk clerk, headed out to Killeen on IH 35 North and then Highway 195 North, a distance of approximately seventy miles, arriving at his destination almost two hours later. He checked into a hotel, making sure it had Wi-Fi availability.

Once he was checked in, Niko turned on his computer and brought up a Killeen street map to locate the Knights' residence. He'd found the address in the old newspaper article with the wedding announcement of Chad and Nora. He found out that the Knights lived in a neighborhood just north of a street named Knight's Way, off Highway 190 West in Harker Heights. Niko saw that the community was not far from where he was staying. He noted the distance and decided to go for a ride and do a little bit of exploring. It was going on seven so it was a perfect time to do a little bit of reconnaissance and also get something to eat. Niko found the small two-bedroom house situated on a large lot with large elm trees in the backyard. He also noticed the house across the street from the Knights was for sale. Perfect! A great idea and the perfect plan came into Niko's fast, calculating mind.

***

That same night, Niko called the real estate agent, a woman by the name of Maria Fuentez, and set up an appointment to see the house the following day, which was a Sunday. At ten in the morning, thirty minutes before the appointed time, Niko was parked, waiting, in front of the house for sale. He wanted to scout the Knights' house and the other houses next to it, as well as the ones across the street. There was no activity in any of the houses until a little past ten, when the Knights came out and started walking away from his parking location.

"Excellent. I would say that this is their regular routine, going for a walk around ten a.m. But let's see what time they return. I think I will ask the agent if she knows if they take their walks daily," said Niko softly to himself.

The agent arrived at ten thirty sharp. "Good morning," she said. "You must be Mr. Stevens. Good to meet you. I am Maria Fuentez."

"Very pleased to meet you," said Niko. "Yes, I am Ted Stevens. And thank you for agreeing to show me the house on a Sunday. I'm short on time and have quite a number of things to accomplish before I head back home."

"No problem, let's go inside the house so you can see it. I always like to start inside and finish by showing the spacious yard. As you can see, all these houses are situated on three-quarter-acre lots with beautiful shade trees. All of these homes were built more than thirty years ago. But don't worry about the foundation or the structure; these houses were built with real lumber, not compressed plywood like today's houses."

"Excellent. I'm scheduled to take a job with the army here at Fort Hood, though I don't report until another thirty days from now. My wife and my two young sons won't be joining me until January of next year, but I'd like to check out the schools as well as the neighbors while I'm here, if we are going to make this our permanent post."

"Well, that's excellent. How old are your children?" asked the agent.

"We have twin boys, both eight years old," said Niko, giggling as he said *both eight years old*. "Now, tell me about the neighbors. I don't want to move into a neighborhood if any of the neighbors are child molesters or predators." He sounded very sincere.

"Oh, no, no!" replied the agent. "Across the street lives a retired army sergeant major and his wife. They'll be excellent neighbors. Both are in their late eighties. No family. Next to them is an active-duty soldier who's almost never home. He's single and I think he does some type of spying work for the army. That's why he's single—in case he gets killed. I don't know if that's true, but that's what I've been told."

"When does he return?"

"He left a couple of days ago and won't return until the middle of next month."

"What about the other two houses, the one next to this house and the other one, next to the sergeant major and his wife?"

"The occupants of the green house next to the Knights—that's the name of the sergeant major—have a teenage girl, but they're on vacation in Colorado as we speak. They left yesterday when I was here showing the house. The other house next to this one is empty and will be put up for sale but it's not on the market yet. The occupants, another Fort Hood soldier and his family, were transferred to Germany," said the agent as she continued walking through the house. She finished showing Niko the inside of the house and they both went outside to view the yard. While Niko and the agent were outside, the Knights walked back to their home.

"Do they always go for walks?" asked Niko.

"Yes, they do, daily."

"Always the same time of day?"

"I believe so."

"I guess that's why they've had a long life," said Niko.

"Well, yes, walking is good for the health as well as the soul," replied the agent.

"If you don't mind, I'd like to take some pictures to take back to my wife and see what she thinks about the house. Is that all right with you?"

"Absolutely," replied the agent.

Niko took out his cell phone and started taking pictures, first of the yard and then of the Knights' house. After he finished, Niko turned to the agent and said, "I'll call you within the week and let you know what my wife thinks of the house, okay?"

"Yes, that would be fine."

"Do you have any other showings scheduled? I don't want you to sell the house before my wife decides."

"No, I don't have any other showings at the present time. So, take your time and don't rush. I tell you what. What if I call you if I get a showing request? Would that help?"

"Oh, yes, it would, and I would really appreciate that."

Niko gave her his phone number and the agent gave him one of her cards. Then they shook hands, said their goodbyes, and went their separate ways. Niko was satisfied he had all the information he needed to complete his holy mission.

Early the next day, Niko went to a drugstore and bought a pair of latex medical gloves. From there, he drove to a hardware store and bought a Stanley medium size screw driver. Then he had breakfast at a small diner not far from the Knights' neighborhood. After finishing breakfast, he went to the house that was for sale and parked his car in front of it. It was nine fifty-five when he got there and, like clockwork, the Knights went out for their daily walk. Niko had timed their walk the day before when he was looking at the house; it had taken the Knights forty-five minutes to return. He waited until the Knights were out of sight and then crossed the street to their residence. He put on the latex gloves and pulled out the screwdriver from his back pocket. Niko went to the back of the house and had no problem opening the kitchen door. But he was surprised to see a Yorkshire terrier, a miniature attack dog, barking and coming straight at him. He kicked the poor animal like a football and then, from one of the drawers next to the sink, pulled out a steak knife and stabbed the barking dog until it stopped moving.

He went through the rooms looking for a toolbox and found one in the pantry. He dug through the toolbox, took out a hammer, went back to where the dog was lying. He smashed the Yorkshire terrier's head with it, praying to Allah with each blow. Niko then went to the front room and waited there for the Knights to return from their morning walk. He saw the couple walking down the sidewalk and quickly went back to the kitchen with the steak knife in his hand. The retired sergeant major unlocked the front door, moving aside to let his wife in. He locked the door once the wife was in the house.

"I wonder where Sparky is," said Mrs. Knight. "He usually meets us at the door."

"He must be asleep in the kitchen after eating what you left for him for his breakfast," replied Mr. Knight.

"You're right," said Mrs. Knight as she walked into the kitchen, where Niko was waiting.

Niko grabbed her, covering her mouth, and ran the knife into her stomach. She started kicking as Niko rammed the knife into her body again and again. In her struggle, she kicked the side of the sink cabinet twice before collapsing.

Mr. Knight heard the noise and asked as he walked towards the kitchen, "Are you okay? Who's making all that racket?"

He entered the kitchen and was surprised by Niko. Niko tried to stab him but the old man still had good reflexes. He threw a right punch to Niko's head but the younger man was able to partially evade the punch, stabbing the old sergeant major twice in the stomach. Mr. Knight threw a second punch, yelling "Camera!" and landing a punch squarely on Niko's jaw, sending him backwards all the way to the front room, where he fell on top of the coffee table. Niko regained his footing and quickly got back up standing in front of the retired sergeant major. Mr. Knight continued to wave the back of his left hand in front of Niko as the younger man stabbed him again several times. Eventually, the old man collapsed. Niko heard Mrs. Knight moving around, went back to the kitchen, and stabbed her one more time. Then he went back to check on the old man. Yes, he was sure both were now dead. He didn't notice that Mr. Knight had taken off his wristwatch when he fell to the floor and put the watch in his trouser pocket before passing out.

Niko took the hammer from the sink countertop and went to work on them. He resumed his praying to Allah with each blow. When he finished, he placed the bloody hammer on the countertop and washed the blood from his gloved hands in the sink. He dried his gloved hands with a towel and then went to the bedroom. There, he found a couple of pictures of Chad and Nora, which he took with him. A few minutes later, Niko walked nonchalantly through the front door and went straight to his car, very proud of having completed his holy mission, saying, *Alhamdulillah*, thanks be to Allah. The neighborhood was empty; there was nobody around to hear or see him. He got in his car, took the gloves off, placed them next to him, and motored back to his hotel, smiling with his Cheshire cat grin.

***

Niko returned to his hotel, looked up available flights to Chicago, checked out of his room after packing, and then headed straight to the airport. He threw the latex gloves and the screwdriver into a trash can as soon as he arrived at the car rental agency. The agency's courtesy van took him to the airport terminal where Niko got on a flight to Chicago. Going to Chicago was a diversionary tactic in case the authorities somehow picked up his trail. He highly doubted that would happen, but still, he wasn't going to take a chance. He would fly from Chicago to Toronto, his home and safe haven.

However, Niko was very mistaken about the safe-haven part. Very soon, he would feel the full wrath of Winters upon him—if the computer hacker didn't get him first.

Chapter 4

Chad returned from London, England, where he'd been assigned to assist the London authorities in the terrorist attacks that took place there. First, it was the Manchester suicide bomber terror attack during the Ariana Grande concert on May 22, 2017, and then the London Bridge stabbing attack on June 3, and finally the Finsbury Park Mosque vehicle terror attack of pedestrians on June 19. Chad closed out his investigations with the British Intelligence Service, commonly known as MI6, on June 29 and returned the following afternoon to Washington, D.C.

Chad did not return to work until July 5 due to the July 4 national holiday—though most of the FBI agents were on duty despite the holiday. He was assigned to assist in the ongoing Russian collusion investigation and was attending an investigative daily briefing by the team leader when he received a call from the acting FBI director.

"Chad, I need to see you immediately in my office. I'm afraid I have bad news for you and I want to personally deliver it to you. Please don't ask me any questions over the telephone."

"Yes, sir. I'll be over within the next thirty minutes, sir."

What bad news could the acting FBI director have? Chad wondered. Did someone in the British Intelligence Service complain about me? He remembered a heated discussion with a senior British Intelligence official on investigative methods but they'd ironed out their differences, so he thought, before he left the MI6 office in London. Is the acting FBI director going to fire me for that or is there another reason? But what other reason could there be? Maybe I'll only get a reprimand and not be fired. These were the thoughts going through Chad's mind as he sped through the Washington, D.C., traffic from the annex to the FBI headquarters.

Chad entered the office of the FBI director and was surprised to see a chaplain in the office as well.

"Chad, I have very sad news for you," the acting director said. "First, this is Chaplain Rogers, a good friend of mine. I took the liberty of inviting him to sit in during our talk. Chad, I received a preliminary report from the police chief in Killeen, Texas. Cletus and Sonia Knight were murdered two nights ago, on July 3. I'm very sorry to tell you that. It seems that it was a home invasion and both of the Knights were killed. I'm very sorry for your loss."

"I don't know what to say," Chad said. "I am sure you know that the Knights are, rather, were what I considered my relatives. They were the parents of the girl I was to marry, who was killed in a shooting in Fort Hood, Texas. After my parents died, the Knights were the only ones left who I considered family. Actually, they were the only family I had. They were both in their eighties. Who would do such a thing to a helpless elderly couple? I'll need time off to go to Killeen and, I suppose, make funeral arrangements. Can I see the report, sir? Are there any suspects?"

"Here's the preliminary police report and, according to the police chief, no, there are no suspects. The police are still investigating the murders. This is a preliminary courtesy report. I'll give you all the time you need to attend to this personal matter, Chad. And if there's anything else you need, let me know. You know you can count on us."

"Thank you, sir. I appreciate that. I went to visit the Knights in Harker Heights in Texas before I left on my London assignment. If you don't mind, sir, I would like to get together with the chaplain and pray for the Knights. They were all I had left in my life after my parents died," said Chad as tears starting running down his cheeks.

Chad went home to pack his traveling bag but soon sat down on the side of the bed and started reminiscing about the many good times he'd had over the years with the Knights. A few moments later, he got up, went to the shelf next to his stereo, and pull out a CD Mr. Knight had given him during his last visit to their home. Mr. Knight told Chad the

CD contained Nora's favorite song, *Unchained Melody*. He put the CD in the stereo and started listening to the various oldies. Then it got to the song by the Righteous Brothers that was Nora's favorite. He turned the stereo volume up to its highest level and starting crying. It was time to let go of his emotions and today was the right time. It was final. He had now lost all of his family.

Chapter 5

Chad got a direct flight from Reagan International to Austin-Bergstrom International Airport in Austin, Texas, and went straight to the police chief's office in Killeen to thank him for the preliminary report and get the address of the mortuary where the bodies were being kept.

"Agent Winters, I would advise you to read the complete report before you go see the bodies at the mortuary," the police chief said.

"Why is that, sir?"

"Because it was a very cruel and gruesome murder. In my opinion, this crime was carried out by a psychopathic individual. It could have been more than one individual, but we believe it was only one person who committed the murder. We are still investigating the crime. Please read the report first, Agent Winters."

Chad took the report from the police chief and sat next to the chief's desk. He started shaking as he read the full report.

"Are you all right, Agent Winters?"

"Yes, I am, sir. It seems we have a lunatic on the loose. He or she smashed their heads with a hammer? Were you able to lift any fingerprints off it?"

"No, we didn't find any prints. The individual must have used gloves. We know the individual broke into the house through the kitchen door because the locked door had been opened with a sharp object. We believe it was only one individual that committed the crime, but that's only speculation. The individual used a hammer from Mr. Knight's toolbox. The first responders found all the tools strewn about in the pantry. We're presently interviewing the neighbors, hoping they might have seen or heard something."

"I would like to join your investigators after I visit the mortuary and the funeral home to make the funeral arrangements. And yes, I will view the bodies to see what this monster did to the Knights. I will not rest until the perpetrator is brought to justice. Thank you, chief. Thank you for your assistance."

"You're welcome, Agent Winters. And again, my condolences. I understand you were engaged to their daughter, but she was killed during a shooting at the base before the wedding a few years ago."

"Yes, sir, that's correct. That was many years ago. Again, thank you, chief. I must be on my way now." And with that, Chad walked out of the chief's office, got in his rental car, and drove to the mortuary where the bodies were being kept.

***

Chad had read the police report so he knew what to expect, but he stood solemnly next to the bodies, devastated. Anger grew in him while he recited two prayers for each of the Knights, who had been, in their own particular way, very religious individuals. Chad remembered Mr. Knight as a strong advocate for the separation of church and state, as written in the US Constitution by the founding fathers. He had further advocated the constitution as a living document that provided equality for all, though he could cite numerous personal stories where this was not upheld. Mr. Knight hated to see interpretations of the bible and the constitution used as political weapons to divide people, especially by the religious right, that resulted in bigotry and prejudice in the name of religious freedom. He always said that the conservative right talks the talk but didn't walk the walk.

And he was very correct on this, Chad thought. Just look at the alleged leader of their political party. He doesn't attend church on a regular basis but only on special occasions or holidays. Prefers to play golf instead. Alleged encounters with prostitutes and other improper sexual behavior without consequences. And he's their conservative political leader? What a joke.

And Mrs. Knight? A loving mother. She was fearless and protective as a lioness, yet gentle as a lamb. Chad remembered a Sunday when he was stationed at Fort Hood and attended mass with Nora and her parents. They were very attentive until the priest talked against same-sex marriage and compared a same-sex couple living together to two bulls being in the same corral. The four of them got up and walked out of the church when they heard the priest use that example in his homily. Mr. Knight felt the reason why good people, especially the young millennials, turn away from church teachings is due to the extreme religious right groups, in their pursuit of political power, deciding morals and values for all people and demonizing those who do not agree with them.

Then Chad's attention shifted back to the cruelty of the crime. It burned inside him and fueled a desire for revenge against the perpetrator. He wanted to administer revenge without any remorse. Chad was ready to unleash a fury of angst and anger on whoever had committed or was involved in this heinous crime. The perpetrator was going to pay dearly. Chad's enormous anger was getting him ready to deliver the worst revenge he could imagine. He finished praying but the anger kept growing inside him. He had to tone it down when the mortuary manager came out of his office and said, "I understand you are the only relative the Knights have, so I want to give you the valuables they had on them when they were brought in. Please follow me, Mr. Winters."

Chad followed the manager to his office and sat down on one of the three chairs lined up in front of the manager's desk. The manager pulled out a small shoebox, opened it, and placed on top of his desk Mr. Knight's wallet, an army ring, a wedding band, and a watch.

"These items belonged to Mr. Knight." Then he placed a set of wedding rings next to Mr. Knight's rings and said, "These rings were Mrs. Knight's."

The manager looked at Chad and said, "You know, the police said it wasn't a robbery because nothing was taken, yet Mr. Knight was not wearing his watch. The watch, which was bloody, was found in his trouser pocket. I understand both of the Knights walked every day at a park near their home. Did he take off his watch after the walk to check the time, or was he trying to hide the watch from the intruder during the attack? How did the watch get bloody if it was in his pocket? I think, and this is me just talking, that he took it off during the attack to hide it from the intruder and that's why the watch was bloody."

"Those are excellent questions and a feasible conclusion, sir," said Chad. "I gave Mr. Knight the watch during my last visit to their home, about two months ago. It's not a regular watch, but a new smartwatch that you talk into. It's the newest thing on the market at the present time. It's a phone, a camera, and much more, rolled into one. I don't even know how to operate it myself, so I will seek assistance from where I purchased it. Thank you for that valuable piece of information. I'm going to call the store for help once I get back to the police chief's office."

Chad thanked the manager again and then headed to the funeral home to make the burial arrangements. After making the funeral arrangements for the following week, Chad took the box with the Knights' belongings and headed out to their residence to see if the investigators were still there and had picked up any clues.

***

Chad got to the Knights' residence and noticed two investigators interviewing an army captain across the street. He stayed in his car until they finished talking to the captain and then stepped out. Chad introduced himself to the two investigators and asked if they'd come up with any clues or evidence.

"No, sir, Agent Winters. The captain you saw us interviewing was on temporary duty and returned home this morning. He lives here by himself. Nobody answered at the green house next to the Knights' and that house across the street that's for sale is vacant. We noticed the for-sale sign across the street and decided to call the real estate agent. We're waiting for her to come by and answer some questions. She told us over the phone she showed the house on Sunday to one individual. First, we want to know if she saw anyone or anything that was suspicious when she was here on Sunday showing the house. And second, we found it odd that someone would be looking at homes for sale on a Sunday, which happens to be the day before the murders. She's coming by in about thirty minutes. Do you want to hang around while we ask her some questions?"

"Yes, I do. But first I'd like to go inside the house and do a walk-through, if you guys don't mind."

"No, we don't. Go ahead, Agent Winters. Who knows, you might come up with something we overlooked."

Chad went into the Knights' house and noticed the broken coffee table in the front room. That indicated to him a struggle had taken place. Did Mr. Knight fall on top of the table or did he hit the perpetrator and the individual fell back and broke the table? Somebody broke the table, that was a given. Chad knew that even though Mr. Knight was in his eighties, he was still pretty strong.

Just then, the real estate agent arrived and got out of her car. Chad decided to go outside and listen to her answers on the sidelines. This was not his investigation; therefore, he was a concerned bystander.

"The last time I was here was on Sunday, July 2, showing the house. I received a call late Saturday from a Mr. Ted Stevens, who said he was pressed for time and asked if I could show him the house on Sunday. He stated he also wanted to check the schools before going back home. He said he was scheduled to start on a new job at the base in about thirty days, but right now he was pressed for time. This is a very quiet and peaceful neighborhood, detective, and no, I saw nothing suspicious going on around the neighborhood while I was here showing the house."

"How often do you get calls to show homes on Sundays?" asked one of the investigators.

"Not often. I've been selling real estate for the past sixteen years and this is the second time that I can recall," replied the agent. "Why? Is Stevens a suspect, detective?"

"No, he's not. We're asking because we find it odd that someone would look at a house on a Sunday. That's all. Just odd."

"What can you tell us about Mr. Stevens? Did he look nervous, suspicious, or angry when you were showing him the house?" asked the other investigator.

"No. He was a smart aleck, though."

"Why do you say that?"

"Because when I asked him about his family, he told me he had twin boys, both the same age, eight years old. He smiled when he said that, with that funny smile of his. He thought it was funny that he said the twins were the same age, but I didn't find it amusing."

"What do you mean, 'with that funny smile of his'?"

"He showed all his teeth when he smiled, like a … what do you call those cats? … a Cheshire cat," she replied. "Well, he did something that was odd, now that you're saying that it's odd to show a house on Sunday. He took some pictures of the Knights' house. He didn't take pictures of the inside of the sale house when we were going from room to room, but only of the yard and the outside of the house. People usually take pictures of the inside of the house. He didn't and I don't think he took pictures of the other houses either, just the Knights'. And he also asked me about the Knights' daily walks. We saw the Knights returning from their walk through the front room window when we were inside the house and he asked me that question."

"Anything else you can remember?" asked the investigator.

"No … Oh, yes! He did ask me if they always went for a daily walk and if it was at the same time. I told him I thought they did. I remember Mr. Stevens asking those questions because he said that it must be the reason for their long lives."

"We would like to have the home address and phone number of Mr. Stevens, if you have it."

"Yes, I do. Let me get the information from my car."

She left the two investigators and Winters standing in the front yard while she retrieved the information on Stevens. After providing them with the home address and telephone number Niko had given her, she left to return to her office.

"We're going to the personnel office at Fort Hood to check out this guy's story out. Want to come along, Agent Winters?" the investigator asked.

"No, but thank you, guys. I'm going to check the smartwatch camera Mr. Knight had in his possession for pictures. I hope he was wearing it during the attack and was able to operate it and take pictures of the attacker. I'll meet you guys tomorrow at the chief's office and we can compare notes." Once the house was secured, the three law enforcement officers went their separate ways.

Early the next day, Chad went to the electronics store in Killeen where he'd purchased the smartwatch and asked the attendant to show him how to retrieve pictures off the watch. The clerk pulled out the memory card, inserted the card into a little gadget connected to a computer, and downloaded all the pictures to a flash drive.

"You follow the same process to download pictures from a smartphone," said the clerk. "Nothing different."

The last four pictures taken that Monday morning were blurry, but Chad knew the pictures could be enhanced by the computers in the FBI headquarters in D.C. Chad went to the police chief's office from the store. The two investigators were in the office.

"We have a suspect, Agent Winters," said the chief. "The personnel office at the base doesn't have any records of a pending hire named Ted Stevens. My investigators also checked the address he gave the real estate agent and it turned out to be bogus. So is the phone number he gave her. We're contacting the real estate agent again and requesting she come in and gave us a full description of this Ted Stevens for a police sketch. I doubt if that's his real name. Did I leave anything out, guys?" asked the chief, turning to the two investigators.

"No, sir," replied the investigators in unison. Chad thanked both investigators as they walked out of the chief's office to continue with the investigation.

"This smartwatch is the one I gave Mr. Knight the last time I visited with them. The watch has a camera and the last four pictures taken seem to be of the perpetrator. I had the pictures downloaded onto a flash drive and saw some of them on the computer screen as they were being downloaded, but they're very blurry. We have a computer in D.C. that can make the pictures clearer, so I'm going to send the flash drive to them," said Chad to the police chief.

"Agent Winters, we have a computer program in our tech center that can do that too. Why don't we take the flash drive with the pictures to the technicians next door and see if they can work on them," said the chief.

"Great! I'll leave the flash drive with you so they can be developed. That will save us a lot of time and maybe we can solve this crime quickly," said Chad, not knowing that this was just the beginning of a long and dangerous journey to find and apprehend the culprit with the Cheshire cat grin.

Chapter 6

Niko arrived at his home in Toronto a couple of days later and quickly sent an email—encrypted, of course—to al-Baghdadi with the news that he had completed the assigned holy mission. He noted in the email that pictures of Chad Winters and Nora Knight, from their early days when they were engaged, were to follow. He also suggested al-Baghdadi publish the story and pictures once he got them.

"I recommend publishing the story, first in our local weekly newspaper, *Al Naba*, to raise the hope and inspiration of our people there," wrote Niko. "And second, run the story with the pictures through the Aamaq News Agency, to serve as validation that an ISIS holy warrior of the caliphate committed the deed in their own backyard."

"Excellent idea. I will publish the story and pictures once I get them," was al-Baghdadi's reply.

***

Chad returned to the police chief's office a couple of days later, after the Knights' funeral, to check on any updates in the murder investigation. The police chief had developed the pictures digitally off the flash drive and gave them to Chad as soon as he arrived. One of the pictures clearly showed the twisted face of the perpetrator falling back away from the old retired sergeant major. So, the intruder was the one who had fallen on the coffee table. The real estate agent's detailed description of Ted Stevens enabled the police artist to draw a sketch that matched, almost perfectly, the picture taken with the smartwatch. While Chad and the chief were looking at the pictures, the chief got a call from the new FBI director looking for Agent Winters.

"Agent Winters, the FBI director wants to talk to you," he said, handing the phone to Chad.

"Yes, sir," said Chad.

"Agent Winters, your cell phone must be off," said the newly Senate-confirmed FBI director, "so I had to call you on the chief's phone."

"Sorry, sir, I turned my phone off while I was at the funeral. The members of my old Army Bravo Team came by to attend the funeral and give me support. They're my army family. We used to take care of each other, especially when we were in the war zones in Iraq and Afghanistan. I hadn't seen any of them for quite a while, so it was nice of them to come and give me support and comfort. They stayed here for a couple of days, going over some of the good times and bad times we had together operating as a team in the army. Their visit was worth a lot to me, sir. I started chitchatting with them and forgot to turn my phone back on. I had my phone off for the past couple of days while they were here. Sorry, sir."

"That's fine, Agent Winters. I called you because we got a tip from one of our undercover agents in Yemen and I wanted to give you a heads-up that all of the major networks are going to carry an ISIS announcement as breaking news. We don't know what they're going to announce, but the tip we got says it concerns the Knights' murders."

"What the hell do they know about the murders?" asked Chad.

"We don't know, but we'll soon find out," replied the FBI director. "Call me after you see the breaking news, Agent Winters."

"Yes, sir. I'll call you. But if you don't mind, sir, please call me Chad."

"Okay, Chad. I'll be waiting for your call," said the FBI director before hanging up.

When Chad arrived, all the police officers from the office—the two detectives assigned to the Knights' murders, plus other detectives and the police chief—were in the conference room with the television on. The news anchor started the breaking news with "The leadership of ISIS released a statement through the Aamaq News Agency and included the following two pictures of FBI Special Agent Chad

Winters and his former fiancée, Nora Knight. ISIS is taking full credit for the brutal murder of the two retirees, the Knights, Nora's parents, in the community of Harker Heights near Killeen, Texas. The ISIS statement reads as follows. 'The murder of retired Sergeant Major Cletus Knight and his wife, Sonia, in Harker Heights, Texas, was carried out by a true believer and holy warrior of the caliphate as a statement that ISIS can hit anytime and anywhere in the United States, the infidel nation. The murders were also carried out to even the score with FBI Agent Winters, who has been a tormentor to our cause.' That's the end of the statement. We are trying to contact Special Agent Winters for comment but the FBI has refused to disclose where he is or comment on the ISIS statement. We'll bring you more news as this story develops."

Chad rose from his seat and started to shake when he saw the pictures of himself and Nora. He knew he was shaking because of his anger. But he was also hurting, hurting really bad deep inside for the Knights. The two detectives assigned to the murder case quickly got up from their seats and placed their hands on Chad's shoulders. Now tears were rolling down his cheeks.

"So, I caused the deaths of the Knights!" exclaimed Chad. "It's because of me they're dead! They've been trying to kill me and failed so they went after the Knights. I won't rest until I get revenge!" He knew he shouldn't be talking about revenge in front of the police officers and quickly composed himself. "I'm sorry, chief, for my display of anger, sir. I lost it for a minute. My apologies, sir, and to everyone else in the room."

"That's okay, Agent Winters. We understand. Nobody blames you for your outburst. It's perfectly normal under these circumstances. We'll find the son of a bitch! I promise you that," said the chief, also showing a bit of anger.

Chad's cell phone rang. The FBI director was calling him.

"Chad, I'm so sorry. Nobody expected to get that type of breaking news story. The murders were carried out as a terrorist attack, so the FBI is taking over this investigation. We'll be notifying the police chief in Killeen that we have jurisdiction over this case. It's ours now. Additionally, I'm assigning Special Agents Lorenzo Lozano and Thomas Reynolds to this case immediately. I understand you know both agents. I want you to return to Washington and keep working on the Russian collusion investigation."

"Sir, I understand your concern," said Chad, "but it's me they want to kill. I would like to be assigned to this case. I've been tracking down al-Qaeda and ISIS sleepers since my first day of employment with the agency. I know how they operate and I'm one of the most experienced agents you have on these two terror groups. Please, let me pursue this case. Additionally, we have a starting point, with a suspect and his picture placing him at the Knights' house."

"Then there's nothing to investigate, Chad. All we have to do is locate and apprehend the individual."

"We have to identify him first and then find him, sir."

"My gut feeling tells me I shouldn't do this, but I'm going to go against my better judgement and assign you to the case. Please be careful, Chad. We know what these guys are capable of doing with no guilt for their actions. I want you to submit regular updates through your supervisor so I can be kept in the loop."

"Yes, sir. I have no problem with that, and thank you, sir. If you want to send Reynolds down, I would appreciate that. He's been my partner since I've been with the agency. Also, I will be scanning the photo of the suspect for identification through our biometric face-recognition system to see if we can identify the person."

"Fax me the photo and we'll start on it immediately," replied the FBI director.

The police chief had been notified by the assistant FBI director, while Chad was on the line with the FBI director, that the agency now had jurisdiction on this terrorist case and Chad would be leading the investigation in Killeen. The police chief quickly assigned the two detectives to assist Chad until his partner, Reynolds, would arrived to join him. In the meantime, Chad sent the two detectives with a photo of the suspect to the hotels and motels located in close proximity to Harker Heights and Killeen.

The detectives got lucky on the third hotel they visited.

"He stayed here, but his name is not Ted Stevens," said the desk clerk. "He registered under the name of Niko Adel Kadyrov from New York City on June 30 and checked out on July 3. That's all the information we have on him."

"Was he by himself or did he have a male or female roommate with him?" asked one of the detectives.

"No, sir. He stayed by himself."

The two detectives returned to the office, where Chad was waiting. They briefed Chad and the police chief on what they'd found out.

"Let's get the real estate agent back here for some additional questioning," said Chad to the two detectives.

The real estate agent came by in less than thirty minutes. Now Chad was the one asking the questions.

"You said that Mr. Ted Stevens called you on Saturday."

"Yes, sir, that's correct."

"Did he call you on your cell phone?"

"Yes, he did."

"Did you call him back?"

"No, I had no reason to call him."

"Do you have your cell phone with you?"

"Yes, I do."

"I'd like to see your calls for July 1, if I may."

The real estate agent handed her cell phone to Chad. He went to the menu and retrieved the July 1 calls. There were nineteen calls on that day, fifteen of them with area code 254, three with area code 972, and one call with area code 416. Chad quickly recognized area code 416 as

Toronto. Area code 254 was Killeen and 972 was Dallas, which was not far away.

"The phone number 262-9388 with area code 416 is from Toronto," said Chad. "I know that because I have the telephone number of the Royal Canadian Mounted Police supervisor with that same area code. There have been quite a number of ISIS sleepers supposedly living in Canada. This character must be one of them. Let's get a judge to grant us permission to get all the calls off his cell phone number from the phone carrier. Our justification for the request will be based on alleged terroristic activities by the suspect. And let's do it immediately. Getting a judge to agree to that should not be a problem."

"Buddy, the carrier for this particular service is in Toronto. Can we get our warrant honored over there?" asked Reynolds, who had arrived earlier that morning to assist in the investigation.

"We'll send the warrant through the diplomatic channels. We'll let the boss figure it out," said Chad.

"Also, let's send a written request to Homeland Security in Washington, D.C., and ask if they have anything in their database on this suspect."

"Agent Winters, we have an email procedure with Homeland Security that will expedite the request process. We can do it electronically and save you valuable time," said the police chief.

"Excellent. We'll go that route then, chief," replied Chad.

Once the police had the name of Niko Adel Kadyrov, now classified as a terrorist by the FBI and a suspect in the murder case, and a fairly good photo of him, an all-points bulletin was quickly put out on the suspect. No luck. The FBI had his cell phone number and were waiting to get a listing from the carrier of all calls made or received on that number. It took almost one week before Homeland Security confirmed via email that a person by the name of Niko Adel Kadyrov, a Canadian citizen, had crossed the US border from Canada and landed at Dulles International Airport. From Dulles, the subject flew to Austin, Texas, and on July 3, flew from Austin to Chicago. From there, he flew back to Toronto on July 7. His home address was 12721 White Lane, Toronto, Canada, and cell phone number, 416-262-9388.

Chad quickly called the Royal Canadian Mounted Police supervisor in Toronto and asked if they would put a tail on the suspect, a Canadian citizen by the name of Niko Adel Kadyrov, until he could get there. He went into detail about why the FBI was looking for this particular person.

"Be glad to oblige, Agent Winters. Oh, by the way, Agent Winters, I recognize the name because he was under surveillance by our intel department some time back. I'll put my best men to follow this character until you get here. I believe we still have his address on file," said the Royal Canadian Mounted Police supervisor. Chad quickly updated the supervisor with the suspect's home address. After he made the call from the chief's office in Killeen, Chad and Reynolds returned to Washington, D.C., to pick up the investigation from there.

***

The Royal Canadian Mounted Police supervisor sent four officers to the address of Niko Adel Kadyrov, but when the Canadian officers arrived at the apartment, they found it empty. Did somebody tip him off?

Chapter 7

Niko was in his apartment a few days later, relaxing after returning from Chicago, when he received a call on his cell phone. The call was from an unidentified individual, who told him he'd been identified by both the FBI and Homeland Security. The caller suggested he get out of Toronto immediately.

"Who is this and how in the hell did you get my cell phone number?" asked Niko, rather angrily. His cell phone showed the call was from a private number.

"Never mind who I am or how I got your number, just consider me your friend, for the time being, who has the same goals as you," replied the caller. "Get out of town before Winters finds you. If he finds you, you'll be history. You brutally murdered the Knights. Winters will take it out on you and in worse ways than what you did to the Knights. The FBI also has your cell phone number, so get rid of your phone. I'm sure they're tracing all of your calls by now and the Canadian police might be monitoring your movements. Take my advice: destroy your cell phone and get out of town now. I suggest you go into hiding until this thing blows over. I know Winters is on his way to Toronto as we speak." With that, the caller hung up.

The conversation gave Niko chills and, for the first time, he felt scared. How in the hell did the FBI find out his identity so quickly and who was this individual on the phone? He called a colleague as soon as the unidentified caller hung up. Niko asked his colleague, who was also a sleeper, to pick him up at his apartment immediately and take him to a certain address that was a safe house in Toronto. His colleague told Niko he would be at his apartment in less than ten minutes. Niko started packing his two large suitcases while he waited, but first he looked out the window to check if he could see anything suspicious outside. Everything looked calm and non-threatening. He decided he would do as the unidentified caller had suggested and immediately go underground to save his ass. Now he was having second thoughts about the mission. He should have declined it, but it was too late for that now.

Niko decided to pray to Allah for forgiveness because he had strayed from the teachings of his religion. It was his fault and now he was paying for it. He had brought this onto himself by indulging in unacceptable Western practices. Maybe it was not too late to ask for mercy and forgiveness from Allah. Niko said, out loud, "*Astaghfiru lillah*," (I seek forgiveness from Allah) while he waited in the safety of his apartment to be picked up, hoping nobody was on his trail yet.

Chapter 8

Chad and Reynolds arrived in Washington, D.C., from Texas and submitted their report to Jackson, their supervisor. They left two days later, arriving in Toronto early in the afternoon. They went straight to the Royal Canadian Mounted Police supervisor's office. Chad again went into detail explaining what evidence the FBI had on the suspect, the gruesome killing that took place as the reason for the investigation of this particular individual, and who the murder victims were.

"I know your men found the apartment empty, but I would like to go by and see where this guy lived. I've got to get a feeling of the person I'm investigating and I want to know everything I can about the individual. I'm sure you are aware that I'm taking this investigation very personally," said Chad to the police supervisor.

"I understand, Agent Winters, and we'll do whatever is needed to help you apprehend this criminal. I am sorry for your loss," said the police supervisor.

The two investigators drove Chad and Reynolds to the suspect's apartment. They had been assigned by the supervisor to assist Chad and Reynolds on this case. Chad had to go over to the apartment, even though he knew it was empty, to make sure Niko Adel Kadyrov wasn't there or hiding nearby. He had to satisfy himself.

They got to the apartment and Chad went to the bedroom, the kitchen, and the small living room, touching every piece of furniture to get a feel for the person who had lived there. He wanted to know everything about the person: his smell, what he ate and drank, anything that could help him apprehend this criminal. He'd already made up his mind that he was going to kill the bastard once he was apprehended. Chad was looking inside the refrigerator when his cell phone rang. It was his supervisor, Jackson, calling him from the FBI office in D.C.

"Chad, we received the listings of all of the calls from the telephone company for the past sixty days with the assistance of the US State Department. The calls stopped three days ago but it's a start. Do I fax you the call list to the Royal Canadian Mounted Police supervisor's office? You gave me his telephone and fax number. Do you want the call list now or do you want to wait until you get back to the office?"

"Please fax the list to the police supervisor's office. There might be some numbers from the surrounding area on the list that we can follow up while we're up here, sir," replied Chad.

"I'll do that immediately."

Chad then had one of the detectives call the police supervisor and give him a heads-up on the incoming fax. After the call, all four left Kadyrov's apartment to return to the office.

The fax was in the police supervisor's office when Chad, Reynolds, and the two detectives got back to the police station. The telephone list contained a large number of calls from the suspect to various phone numbers. Chad went back to the July 1 calls, starting off with the suspect's call to the real estate agent. He noticed that the second-to-last call on the list was received from a private number and the last call made was to a Toronto number with the area code 416. Both calls were made on the same day and minutes apart; nothing followed after those two calls.

"Let's get the name and address on this Toronto number," said Chad to one of the detectives.

"Yes sir. I'll call the cell phone company and get the information for you, sir. The company is located not too far from here," replied the detective.

"The suspect got a call on that same day but from a private number. Is there any way we can identify the number and get the same information on it?" asked Chad.

"No, sir, but we can try and see what information we can get on the private number from the cell phone company."

"I'd appreciate whatever information you can get," replied Chad.

It was around noon when the information on the last number called came in.

"Sir, the number belongs to a Rama Abu Ramadi and here's his home address," said one of the detectives.

It was late in the afternoon when Chad, Reynolds, and the two detectives went to the home of Ramadi. He'd been on the Royal Canadian Mounted Police's radar two years earlier but had also been dropped off the surveillance list. The two Canadian detectives forced open the door and all four individuals rushed in, weapons drawn. They found Ramadi asleep in his bedroom with a young woman, both in the nude.

"Stay where you are, Ramadi, and don't make a stupid move!" yelled one of the detectives.

The young woman started yelling and cursing in French, grabbed a pillow, and placed it in front of her, covering her body.

"Who the fuck are you?" yelled Ramadi.

"Royal Canadian Mounted Police and these two gentlemen are from the United States. They're FBI Agents," said one of the detectives.

"You have no right to burst into my apartment like this!"

"Shut up and get dressed! You're going downtown to answer some questions," said the other detective.

"Why? I haven't done anything wrong!"

"We need to know what you know about Niko Adel Kadyrov."

"I don't know anyone by that name," said Ramadi.

"Yes, you do," said Chad. "He called you on July 15. Where did you take him, Ramadi?" he asked, moving closer to Ramadi, not knowing if the second part of his statement was true. When Chad got real close, he grabbed Ramadi by the throat and said, "You will tell me everything you know, understand, fuckhead? And if you don't, I will make your fucking life miserable!"

"Easy, Chad," said Reynolds. "Turn him loose and let's get him dressed so we can question him in the supervisor's office."

"Sorry, buddy, I'm a little tense."

They had a warrant for the arrest of Ramadi but nothing for the girl, so they had to let her go after she answered a few questions. It turned out she was a call girl and had met Ramadi earlier that day at a designated place where she was picked up for paid-sex services. She went to the bathroom, got dressed, and quickly left the apartment, scared and crying as she hurriedly walked out the door. The two detectives held Ramadi at gunpoint while he got dressed. Chad and Reynolds searched the apartment for any incriminating evidence they might find. They had no such luck, so all four left the apartment, taking Ramadi in handcuffs back to the police station for intense questioning.

It was late at night when Ramadi finally broke down and told them what he knew. "Okay, okay! Niko called me and asked if I would go to his apartment and pick him up. I did what he asked and then I drove him to St. Dennis Drive near the Darul Khair Islamic Centre. He didn't tell me where he was going, for security reasons. If I don't know where he went from there, then I can't tell you. I swear that's the honest truth. I know he destroyed his cell phone right after he called me, so he couldn't be tracked. That's all I know," said Ramadi.

"You haven't talked to him since then?' asked Chad.

"That's correct. He has no cell phone, so I have no way to contact him."

"How did he know to call you?" asked Reynolds.

"We grew up together in Uzbekistan."

"Where in the hell is that?" asked Reynolds.

"It's in Central Asia, north of Afghanistan. We lived in the same neighborhood in Tashkent, the capital," replied Ramadi.

"So, you two grew up together?" asked Chad.

"Yes. We're old friends. We immigrated together to Canada about twenty years ago. We sometimes socialize together and meet up at different clubs."

"Give us the names of his other friends here in Toronto and elsewhere in Canada. You should know his friends if you two have known each other for more than twenty years," said Chad.

"I don't know any of his friends," replied Ramadi.

"We both know that's bullshit, Ramadi. You guys have been friends for that long and you're telling me you don't know any of his friends? I'm going to give you one chance, and only one. You either give me that information or you'll be very sorry," said Chad, standing up and towering over Ramadi while grabbing him again around his throat.

"I think I know a few of his friends. I know their names but I don't have their addresses. I might have the phone numbers of some of them," said Ramadi.

"Good answer," said Chad, releasing his grip on Ramadi's throat. "Now start talking, asshole!"

They held him for approximately four hours and it was close to one in the morning when they decided to let him go, but only after Ramadi had provided Chad with a list of names and phone numbers.

"Okay, you're free to go," said one of the Canadian detectives.

"Who's going to take me home?" asked Ramadi.

"What the hell do you think we are, a taxicab company? You take a fucking cab, bus, or walk! Now get the hell out of here before I kick your ass out!" said one of the detectives.

Ramadi walked out of the police station and, once outside, said in a very low voice, "Bunch of assholes..." and started walking to some taxicabs parked nearby.

"Let's keep an eye on him," said Chad to one of the detectives.

"We'll do that, sir. We also have the equipment to listen to his conversations and monitor his movements inside his apartment. Incidentally, the complex across the street belongs to a close friend of the police supervisor. I told the boss where Ramadi lived after we picked him up and finished questioning him. All you have to do, Agent Winters, is have the police supervisor give his friend a call to get an apartment with a good view of the suspect's apartment. Once we have it for our use, we can put a monitoring plan into action."

"Let's do it," replied Chad. "I'll talk to the police supervisor."

After a week of interviewing Niko's alleged friends, Chad and Reynolds were disappointed that no one provided any useful information on Kadyrov. Some claimed they didn't even know him.

"Well, at least the people Ramadi turned in as Niko's friends didn't turn up dead, like in our previous investigation of Sami Walters," said Reynolds.

"That's what bothers me," said Chad.

"What? That they weren't killed?"

"Exactly. Ramadi gave us names of individuals that really don't know shit about Niko. Some claimed they don't even know him. He gave us names only to lead us on a wild goose chase. Ramadi knows more than he told us. Let's get back to him and really pressure him for good information. He gave us crap."

Chad and Reynolds went to the apartment with the perfect view, where the officer was keeping an eye on Ramadi across the street. The apartment had been equipped by the police with a high-powered telescope and listening equipment.

"He's been in his apartment all day, sir," said the officer assigned as the tail and monitor. "He went to work yesterday, went out to lunch, returned back to work, and afterwards went directly to a bar and then back home. That's been his regular routine for the past few days. He hasn't had any visitors either or made any phone calls while in his apartment. He hasn't left the apartment since he came in this morning, a little past midnight. Seems like he didn't go to work today."

That got Chad worried. He rushed across the street to Ramadi's apartment, accompanied by Reynolds and the police officer. Reynolds knocked on the door but got no answer. Chad decided to get the manager to open the door, as this was a police matter. The manager opened the door. As they entered the apartment, Reynolds called out Ramadi's name, but got no answer. Reynolds went to the kitchen while Chad entered the bedroom. There was a person in bed, a sheet covering the face. Chad pulled the sheet away and saw it was Ramadi. Was he dead?

"Damn it! Somebody call an ambulance! Ramadi is here but it looks as if he's dead!" yelled Chad. The police officer quickly called for an ambulance to pick up Ramadi.

Ramadi was taken to the hospital, where the emergency room physician declared him dead.

"He has no body marks, so my guess is that Ramadi was poisoned," said Reynolds.

"Well, I'm going to request an autopsy," said Chad glumly, remembering the turmoil his last autopsy request in Canada had caused with his supervisors. During that previous episode, he and Reynolds had been after a prime suspect in the murder of a US congresswoman. The suspect was found dead by the Royal Canadian Mounted Police, on a snow-covered golf course in Toronto, shot in the back of the head. An open-and-shut case, according to the Canadian police supervisor present at the scene. Chad had his suspicions and decided to ask for an autopsy instead. When the Canadian medical examiner sent the autopsy invoice to the FBI, Chad was chastised because of the amount of the bill. A few days later, the full autopsy report came in, indicating that the victim had been poisoned before being shot. The poisoning of the victim opened an investigative prospect for both Chad and Reynolds to follow as a lead, bringing accolades to Chad for being proactive in that case.

Early the next morning, both went back to the office to continue checking the telephone list from the cell phone company. The autopsy report came in later that day with the information that Ramadi had been poisoned, just as Reynolds had predicted. The medical examiner's report said his body contained traces of arsenic trichloride, a poisonous liquid.

"We need to find out how the arsenic got into his body and who did it. Let's go to his apartment and do some checking. And while we're there, let's get the apartment's security camera footage. We'll start reviewing the footage from the day we picked him up. We might be able to determine if someone went into his apartment," said Chad.

"Great idea, buddy," replied Reynolds.

They got the security camera from the apartment manager and started reviewing the footage in the privacy of the apartment manager's office. What they saw on the security footage surprised them.

"Okay," said Chad, "we have this old man going into Ramadi's apartment the day before we found him dead. Now, if you look carefully, you can see it's not an old man but someone disguised as an old man. Is it Niko Adel Kadyrov walking into Ramadi's apartment? Is he the killer? He's carrying a six-pack of Coke bottles as he goes into the apartment. Then he leaves, approximately seven minutes later, with the six-pack and a large black plastic bag. Is that the same six-pack he carried into the apartment? And what's he carrying in the plastic bag? He's wearing gloves and has a key to the apartment. Remember that Ramadi said they were good friends. Good enough friends that Kadyrov had a key to Ramadi's apartment? Let's go check Ramadi's refrigerator and see what we find."

They walked out of the manager's office, thanking him for the use of his private office. Then they went to Ramadi's apartment, going straight to the refrigerator. Inside the refrigerator, Chad found a six-pack carton with two unopened soda bottles and four empties in a small plastic trash can underneath the sink.

"Well, we know he wasn't carrying the trash in the black plastic bag," said Reynolds. "All the trash is still here."

They took all six bottles back to the police lab for analysis, as well as a small laptop computer and a spiral notebook with some notes written in Arabic and another foreign language. Two of the empty bottles contained traces of the arsenic, substantiating the fact that Ramadi had been poisoned. Arsenic was also found in the two unopened soda bottles.

"Whoever did it, Agent Winters, took their sweet time preparing the sodas with the poison. Notice the tiny pin-size hole in the bottle caps. The individual used a syringe to extract about one fluid ounce of soda and replaced it with the arsenic poison. You are dealing with a person who goes to great lengths to accomplish the things he sets out to do," said the medical examiner to Chad and Reynolds and the Royal Canadian Mounted Police supervisor, who had come in and was standing next to them.

"Sir, do you have someone in your office who can check the laptop for possible leads and also someone to translate the notes in the spiral notebook? I know some notes are in Arabic, but I can't tell about the other ones. Can you have someone look into that?" asked Chad, directing his question to the police supervisor.

"I'll see what I can do, Agent Winters."

"Where in the hell do all these crazies hide? And who's financing these terrorists here in Canada?" Chad looked at Reynolds while asking the question.

"Let's start with the money trail," replied Reynolds. "That, to me, looks like a good starting point. Follow the money."

"I agree with you. We'll subpoena both Ramadi's and Kadyrov's bank records and see if we can find something there. We can subpoena the bank records here in Canada, can't we, sir?" Chad asked the police supervisor.

"You're damn right we can do that, Agent Winters. I'll start the paperwork for the request immediately."

It took two days for the Royal Canadian Mounted Police to get the bank records on both individuals. It seemed that every individual in Toronto did their banking with the biggest bank in Toronto, making it easy for the Canadian police to find the accounts of both Ramadi and Kadyrov on their first try. Chad and Reynolds were going over the bank records when Reynolds asked, "What's bothering you, buddy?"

"The second-to-last call on Kadyrov's cell phone list. That's what's bothering me right now. It's from a private number. We know the last call made by Kadyrov was to Ramadi. It seems that someone called Kadyrov and possibly gave him a heads-up before the police got to his apartment. Someone who knew we were looking for him but didn't want Kadyrov to know who was calling. That's why the number shows up as a private number. The question is, who called him? The number will show up as a private number when the caller enters star-67 and then the number they're calling. The person receiving the call sees on their cell phone a call coming in from a private number. That keeps the identity of the caller secret. Kadyrov, himself, most likely doesn't know who called him. There's no way the telephone company can decipher the private number either, unless the person receiving the call has an app on their phone that can do that when the call is initially received. Who knew we were looking for Kadyrov besides us?"

"I don't really know, buddy. Who knew we were looking for him?" asked Reynolds.

"Well, the cell phone carrier for one, the Killeen police department, us, the FBI, the Canadian police, and Homeland Security. Where's the mole that possibly gave Kadyrov a heads-up? I'm going to eliminate the Killeen police department and the FBI. The request for information on Kadyrov went to the cell phone carrier when we requested the call list and to Homeland Security when we requested Kadyrov's information, which are outside sources. The Canadian police supervisor stated that both Ramadi and Kadyrov had been under surveillance by his department at one time but that the surveillance on both individuals was dropped. Why was it dropped, is the question. We need to ask the police supervisor that question. Also, let's find out who handled the request at the cell phone carrier and the same at Homeland Security. The carrier provided us with Kadyrov's cell phone calls and Homeland Security with his flight itinerary. I'll bet the mole is in one of those two entities."

"So, the mole that called Kadyrov is in one of those two entities?"

"No, that's not correct. I'm getting ahead of myself. The cell phone carrier didn't know we were looking for Kadyrov until after that private number called him. The private number shows up on the call list before we requested the phone call records. I believe the call from the private number was made to Kadyrov after we sent out the request to Homeland Security for Kadyrov's information. That leaves only Homeland Security as the source of the mole. Let's find out who handled the request there and also ask the police supervisor why the surveillance by his police department was dropped. With luck, we might find the mole and, hopefully, Kadyrov."

"Wow! You do have your thinking hat on, don't you, buddy?" said Reynolds, impressed with the analytical thinking Chad had used to arrive at his conclusion, though they still could not connect all the dots.

"Let's find out the name of the individual who handled the request at the cell phone carrier to make double-sure we're on the safe side. We've got to cover all bases. The private number call was made before we requested the phone records but we still don't want to overlook anything. Records and dates can be manipulated and changed. We need to make sure the call dates were not changed. The carrier is here in Toronto, so we can handle that ourselves, but first, let's run it past Jackson and see what he thinks about us questioning DHS for a possible mole."

"Good idea, buddy. Do we stop checking the bank statements?"

"For the time being," said Chad. "Let's call Jackson at headquarters and then talk to the police supervisor about the surveillance and why it was stopped. Then we'll have the police supervisor call the bank and freeze both accounts until we can resume the review. We'll also instruct the bank to advise the police supervisor if there's an attempt to withdraw the money. The funds should be frozen and the bank shouldn't let the money be withdrawn. Once we do all of that, we'll go out and visit the cell phone provider."

"Okay, let's do it," replied Reynolds.

***

Chad had to postpone his meeting with the police supervisor because of a conflict in the supervisor's schedule. So, he and Reynolds went to the cell phone carrier's office to find out who had processed the request for Kadyrov's cell phone call record.

"Yes, sir, the employee who processed the request is Nellie Chong. I'll take you to the cubicle where she works. Please follow me, sir," said the supervisor. They walked over to her cubical.

"Ms. Chong, these two gentlemen would like to talk to you about the request for Mr. Kadyrov's record of cell phone calls. They're with the Federal Bureau of Investigations, the FBI from the United States. Please answer all of their questions without hesitation, Ms. Chong."

"Yes, sir, I will do that," replied the young employee.

After about forty-five minutes of questioning, Chad was convinced Ms. Chong was not the mole. She had answered all of their questions truthfully. Chad and Reynolds thanked the supervisor and Ms. Chong and headed back to the police supervisor's office.

"Yes, Agent Winters, we dropped the surveillance on both individuals about two years ago because of limited funds. We couldn't keep paying the private contractor to keep the surveillance going after a certain length of time. Our budget couldn't sustain payment for the surveillance after so many months," said the police supervisor.

"You had the surveillance contracted out to a private contractor?" asked Chad.

"Yes, sir, we did. The contractor was recommended to us by your Department of Homeland Security. I'm sure the contractor, as well as the contractor's employees, were vetted by Homeland Security, or else they wouldn't have recommended them to us," replied the police supervisor.

"I would hope so," said Chad. "I need you to provide me with the name of that contractor. He might still be doing contract work with DHS and, if so, we need to check the contractor's employees. I believe someone tipped Kadyrov off that we had identified him and that was the call he received from the individual with the private number."

"I think you're correct, Agent Winters. The contractor doing the surveillance, Boles and Tinsel, had all the information on both Kadyrov and Ramadi. I was informed by your DHS that the contractor and their employees go through some type of orientation program before they send them out to the field."

"Then we have to pay DHS in Washington, D.C., a visit and get as much information as we can get from them," said Chad. "Oh, before I forget, can you request the bank put a hold on both accounts until we can review them? Can you do that for us, sir?"

"I took the initiative to request they freeze the funds when I initially requested the individuals' bank records, Agent Winters. They are to advise me if there's any attempt to withdraw the funds," the police supervisor responded.

"Excellent, sir. You should be commended for doing that," replied Chad.

Chapter 9

Niko was stunned when he heard the breaking news on TV and read in the newspapers that Ramadi, his childhood friend, had been poisoned in his apartment. There were no suspects, according to the police, but the investigation by both the Royal Canadian Mounted Police and the FBI was continuing.

"Who would have poisoned Rami?" Niko asked himself, referring to Ramadi by the nickname he'd used during their early years growing up together in Tashkent. The death of Ramadi got Niko scared. He had to be on the lookout for Winters, knowing that Winters was out to kill him, but now who else was out there? Who killed Rami? Was he in danger from this unknown killer too? He knew who Winters was and what he looked like, but he had no idea who the unknown killer was. Was the killer coming after him too? The killer had known where Ramadi lived, so he had to stay hidden. Who could he trust? Why was Ramadi killed? Was the killer a close acquaintance of both him and Ramadi? The more questions he had with no answers, the more scared he became. Was he really safe staying here with Zarif?

Niko finally went to sleep in the one-room basement apartment owned by Zarif Abdulin, his friend from Uzbekistan, who was also an ISIS sleeper and had been living in Canada for at least fifteen years now. He lived with his voluptuous girlfriend, Madina.

Flag of Uzbekistan

***

Masoud Mohtaat was a trained computer programmer, as well as a chemist, who had sharpened his computer-hacking skills while working at a Russian troll farm in the Kremlin's infamous Yellow Building in Moscow. Mohtaat had been an early contributor to the development of the software that became known as the Kaspersky Lab software, now being used by the industry worldwide. The troll farm was owned and operated by the former KGB, presently known as the Federal Security Service, in Russia, where Mohtaat had trained intensively at an early age. After his training, he returned to his native country of Afghanistan and took up chemical engineering to further his education before eventually immigrating to Canada shortly after the US invasion of Afghanistan in 2001.

He had been tracking both Kadyrov and Ramadi for the last couple of years through their computer keystrokes and intercepted email responses. He had entered their apartments when they were not at home, made molds of their extra apartment keys, and downloaded the SpyMaster Keystroke Shot, a spyware program that showed, on a remote computer, the keystrokes typed before email messages were encrypted on their laptop computers. The program was also capable of intercepting in-coming emails, even if they were encrypted, and routing them to his computer, operating in complete stealth. Mohtaat read the intercepted emails once they were decrypted, so he knew what they were up to—all from the comfort of his home.

His intentions at the present time were strictly financial. He knew that both individuals had received money from al-Qaeda, ISIS, or the Taliban in Eastern Afghanistan to carry out their holy missions in the United States. The Taliban made their money, and lots of it, off the opium trade in Afghanistan. The opium trade had increased by five thousand percent since the invasion by the United States in 2001. That's where the Taliban got the money to support terrorist activities in all parts of the Middle East. Mohtaat was upset when he read the email from al-Baghdadi's supposed assistant advising Niko that a large amount of money had been deposited into his bank account. Mohtaat was a practicing and devout Muslim and considered the acceptance of money for carrying out a holy religious mission a deadly sin. He considered the carrying out of holy Muslim missions to be the unpaid responsibility of every Muslim male. Getting paid for carrying out this responsibility angered Mohtaat, a proud holy warrior from the city of Kabul, Afghanistan.

Flag of Afghanistan

"Why should these faithless Uzbekistanis be receiving this money for carrying out their lawful religious duty under Islamic law? Paying them money to carry out their religious duty is a deadly sin and shows disrespect for Islam as far as I'm concerned. Next, will they be getting paid to attend prayer service at a mosque?" a very angry Mohtaat asked himself.

Mohtaat had lived in Toronto going on fifteen years. He was known in Canada by his Afghan name, Masoud Mohtaat, and was a Canadian citizen in good standing. That meant that he had never been arrested or charged with any Canadian law violation. But for traveling and employment purposes, Mohtaat went by the name of Alfred Robinson, which was on a fake Canadian passport he'd obtained from a criminal Canadian source. He also had a fake diploma from the University of Canada acknowledging the bestowment of a degree in computer programming. He was an itinerant, traveling all over Canada and even into the United States whenever he had the opportunity to execute a holy mission with his fake Canadian passport. And executing a holy mission was his own doing. He didn't need any prodding or financial payment from anyone, only the spiritual desire to help, which came from his heart, from his faith and respect for his religious convictions.

Mohtaat had considered Ramadi an idiot since the first day he started tracking him as part of his subcontractor work with Boles and Tinsel. Today, Ramadi proved him correct. He had received twenty-five thousand dollars from the al-Qaeda leader, Doctor Ayman al-Zawahiri, about one year ago. Mohtaat was unsure if Ramadi had performed a holy mission for that amount of money, but that didn't matter anymore. He found out that Ramadi had recently withdrawn the full amount and hidden the money somewhere in the house. Mohtaat found it hidden under the mattress after he left the poisoned sodas in Ramadi's refrigerator. Ramadi was such an idiot. Now the twenty-five thousand dollars belonged to him. He had dressed as an old man when he went into Ramadi's apartment to leave the poisoned sodas, knowing that the apartment security cameras would get him on film. The time had arrived to eliminate Ramadi once he found out the Canadian police and agents from the FBI had questioned him. Ramadi had sent an email to Kadyrov, which Mohtaat had intercepted, telling him the police had questioned him but that he didn't tell them anything of value. Mohtaat didn't know how much Ramadi had said to the authorities, but whatever he told them was still too much. Say your prayers to Allah, Ramadi, poor faithless bastard, he had thought, it's time for you to answer to Him.

Stealing the money from Kadyrov, though he didn't know how much Kadyrov had received, was going to be slightly more difficult. The money had been deposited directly into Kadyrov's bank account and, as far as he knew, was still in the bank. He knew this because Kadyrov hadn't accessed his bank account since the deposit. Large bank deposits were usually not reported by the banks to the Canadian government, which was not the case in the United States. Here in Canada, you could get away with it.

Mohtaat had a problem, though not a major one. Kadyrov had gone into hiding and he really didn't know if Kadyrov was still in Toronto or had gone to some other city in Canada. The only thing to do was wait, have patience, and hope that Kadyrov would use his laptop so he could, once again, track his computer keystrokes and hopefully find him, eliminate him, and take his money, *insha Allah* (God willing).

Chapter 10

Chad and Reynolds flew back to Washington, D.C., from Toronto to pick up the investigation from there. After conferring with the FBI director, the assistant FBI director, and their immediate supervisor, Sam Jackson, all agreed with Chad's suggestion, giving him their approval to go to the Department of Homeland Security office in Washington, D.C., to check the employees of the private contractor, Boles and Tinsel. Chad was afraid he was going to encounter another Snowden-type employee in the contractor's ranks.

At DHS, Chad and Reynolds talked to the supervisor who had recommended Boles and Tinsel to the Canadian police for the contract surveillance work.

"We vetted the contractor for that surveillance work. But we leave it up to the contractor himself to do the police check, background check, drug check, credit check, and all that good stuff before they hire their employees, Agent Winters."

"So, you don't vet the contractor's employees, then?" asked Chad.

"Well, like I said—"

"I know what you said, sir. My question is, do you vet the employees, and the answer seems to be no."

"That is correct. We don't, but you have to understand, Agent Winters, we don't have the funds to vet contractors' employees. We leave it up to the contractor."

"I understand the contractor and his employees, once recommended by DHS to an outside agency for hire, go through some type of orientation program run by your staff here in your office before they go out in the field. Is that correct, sir?"

"Yes, sir, that's correct."

"How long is that orientation and what does it consist of? Can you explain the process to me, sir?"

"It's one-week long and consists of reporting procedures from the field using our forms report program. We give them a disk with the unclassified program to download onto their laptops here in our computer laboratory. They fill out the program forms on their computers and then they're supposed to send them back to us via the computer. All of that information goes into our database. However, we never got any reports from them. We followed up with the Royal Canadian Mounted Police, but we were told they'd dropped the surveillance on the subjects."

"I see," replied Chad. "Is this where our request for information on our suspect, Kadyrov, came to?"

"Yes, sir."

"Who handled that request here in your office?" asked Chad.

"The special requests person. She's working on that computer over there, doing reporting work or answering requests from the field such as the one that the Killeen police chief submitted on your suspect."

"Can we walk over there, so I can see the work area and possibly ask her a couple of questions?"

"Sure, of course you can, Agent Winters. Follow me, please."

Mary, the special requests person, was an employee transfer from another agency. She had transferred to secure a higher pay grade with DHS.

"Mary, these two gentlemen are with the FBI. Agent Winters here wants to see your computer and ask you some questions. Go ahead, Agent Winters," the supervisor said.

"Thank you, sir," Chad responded. "Hello, Mary. Sometime last month, you processed a request for information from the Killeen, Texas, police department on a person by the name of Niko Adel Kadyrov. Do you remember processing that request, Mary?"

"Yes, sir, I do. It's a weird name because when you change the K to an L, it becomes Ladyrov, the main character in a horror movie I once saw when I was growing up. I still remember that scary movie very well."

"That's good, Mary. I think I'll start doing that type of name association so I can remember names. Now, let me ask you another question. How often do you run a scan on your computer for malware, viruses, and things like that?" asked Chad.

Mary looked at her supervisor and hesitated for a moment but finally answered in a rather embarrassed way, "I've been here going on three years now and we haven't done any."

"What are you driving at, Agent Winters?" asked the puzzled supervisor.

"That you let the contractor's employees, and we don't know if they were vetted, come in here and download your form reports program onto their laptops. Were the contractor's employees under someone's supervision when they downloaded your forms program onto their computers?"

"I don't really recall, Agent Winters," replied the supervisor.

"Then we don't know if someone loaded something onto Mary's computer. I recommend that you immediately run a check on all of your computers to make sure nothing was downloaded onto them. Maybe someone downloaded some malware virus or Mary opened an email that was infected. I recommend you do a thorough check, especially on Mary's computer, immediately. A few years back, we confiscated a laptop from a Middle Eastern terrorist, but we couldn't open his emails. It was by accident that one of the computer operators hit the delete key, opening the email message we wanted open. The terrorist had programmed the computer not to open the email messages unless the delete key was entered first. Now, a trained computer operator would never hit the delete key unless they wanted to delete something, right?"

"That's correct, but we don't have any classified information on these computers, Agent Winters. This particular computer here that Mary uses is used to send out—" He didn't finish the sentence. "Shit! Are you saying someone might have loaded a malware program or somehow Mary's computer got infected and someone can get her stuff off her computer?"

"Yes, sir, that's more or less what I believe we have here. Now, let me ask you one other question. What computer program do you use on your computers?" Chad asked.

"The government-approved Kaspersky Lab software. Why?"

"The FBI is suspicious of that particular software because it has ties to the Kremlin. Actually, it's owned by them. They can very easily put a virus in the program that will be activated when you hit certain computer keys. That's what we were told once in an FBI computer safety seminar conducted by our own cyber-security threat division personnel. Additionally, we learned that Russia has been hacking our domestic energy companies, specifically our electrical grid, since 2016. Mary, what information did you put in the email that you sent back to the Killeen police chief? Do you remember?"

"I can bring up the response I sent from my email's sent folder and tell you."

"Okay, do that, but don't type anything else until we check your computer for malware, or rather for a spyware virus program," said Chad.

Mary brought up the email. It read: "As requested by FBI Special Agent Winters and the Killeen police department, the following information is what DHS has on a Niko Adel Kadyrov: subject crossed the US border from Canada and landed in Dulles International Airport. From Dulles, the subject flew to Austin, Texas, and on July 3, flew from Austin to Chicago. And from there, he flew back to Toronto, Canada, on July 7. The subject is a Canadian citizen. Home address: 12721 White Lane, Toronto, Canada, and cell phone number 416-262-9388. Please let me know if I can be of further assistance."

Chad was now certain that was how the caller with the private number got Niko Kadyrov's cell phone number, if he didn't have it before. Somehow, that individual got the information from Mary's computer, though Chad still didn't know how that had been accomplished.

The DHS supervisor called their tech department for assistance. Once the computer specialist ran an anti-malware program on Mary's computer, he found out it been compromised. The computer specialist stated that Mary's computer had the program SpyMaster Keystroke Shot, a program that transfers the keystrokes to a remote computer. Now Chad knew how the private number caller had acquired the number. But he still didn't know how that program got onto Mary's computer. Did someone download the spyware program or did the virus infect the computer when an external message was opened? Nobody had the answer at the moment, but everything pointed to the spyware program being in Mary's computer for illegal information-gathering purposes.

"It will take me a minute to clean the computer and eliminate the threat," said the computer specialist.

"No," said Chad "leave the spyware program on her computer. I believe someone is remotely reading Mary's keystrokes. I say that the individual is not interested in anything except emails concerning terrorist activities coming under investigation by DHS. That's my guess. We can use it to try to find the individual by sending out fake messages for him to read, if my hunch is correct. I would recommend you isolate this computer and not use it until we get an opportunity to use it as a counter-tool. And let's hope this is the only computer infected. Are you agreeable to that, sir?"

"Yes, I am. We will isolate the computer and not use it, and it will be here until you need it for your use, Agent Winters. We'll give Mary a new computer. And we'll check all of the other computers for spyware as well," replied the supervisor.

"Okay, next, give us a listing of all Boles and Tinsel employees. Maybe one of them downloaded the spyware program on Mary's computer when they went through your orientation program. Otherwise, Mary's computer got infected when she opened an email message coming from an external source," said Chad.

The list consisted of six Boles and Tinsel employees, all residents of Canada: James Littleson, William Pickle, Lawrence Whitney, Alfred Robinson, Abel Suttles, and Margaret Grimms. They checked the DHS database while they were there, but nothing suspicious came up on any of the six employees. Actually, there was no record of any of the individuals in the DHS database.

Well, at least Chad and Reynolds now knew how the private number caller got the information on Kadyrov. Was one of the employees who tipped him off? Did they have the same information on Ramadi? Chad wasn't sure, but there was no telling what these characters were capable of doing. Maybe the private number caller killed Ramadi. If he did, why? Chad and Reynolds left the DHS office and went home to prepare to fly back to Canada the next day. No sense working late in the DHS **office** in Washington, D.C., since Chad and Reynolds were not at liberty to work late in someone else's office, especially when everyone else would be going home at exactly four thirty in the afternoon.

Chapter 11

Niko was more upset than worried. He felt he was a prisoner in his own home, although he was hiding in the basement of the house of one of his most trusted friends in Toronto. His friend's house was located in a multicultural neighborhood in Koreatown, making it easy for him and his friend to blend in among neighbors of many different ethnicities. This was an excellent neighborhood to hide in, where he wouldn't raise any suspicion. But, as you could tell by its name, the main ethnic group in this particular neighborhood was Korean.

Niko kept asking himself why this holy mission had turned into such a fiasco. Was this his punishment by Allah for not being a true believer? He didn't think so, but it had crossed his mind. Niko quickly decided to get those punishing thoughts out of his mind and think about how he was going to get out of Canada if Winters was looking for him. But where would he go? To Chechnya, his nation of birth? Why not? The holy mission had been completed as far as he was concerned, so why stay here if his life was in danger? He had computer skills that he could barter with the government of Chechnya. And most importantly, wasn't he related to the president of that country? He sure was. So, he decided, Chechnya was the country he was going to go to. In the meantime, he was going to stay with Zarif, his trusted Canadian friend, for his own safety.

Niko met his friend Zarif while growing up in Uzbekistan. He was his roommate when both were in a private school in that country. Zarif had resided in Canada since arriving here some fifteen years ago. He would provide Niko shelter until he could get back on his feet and, hopefully, get out of Canada. Money was not a concern; he still had the large deposit in his bank account. Then he started thinking about how to get the money out of Canada. He had a Chechen friend he'd met on one of his many visits to his nation of birth. All he had to do was advise this friend that a large amount of money would be transmitted to his Chechen bank account for safekeeping until he got there, so he would need his bank account and the routing number for the transfer. He couldn't take the money with him on his flight to Chechnya, if he was going there, because that large sum of money would have to be declared with Immigrations and that would be a major problem. Having worked out the money problem in his head, he set out to type the email to his Chechen friend on his laptop, requesting his account number and the routing number for the transfer. He also included in the email when his friend should expect to receive the money and the name of the bank it was coming from and explained the reason for the transfer. Big, big mistake. Somebody was reading Niko's email on a remote computer as he composed it.

Chechnya

***

Masoud Mohtaat was sitting on a *toshak* in his luxury apartment, drinking a glass of Afghan mint tea when he heard his computer alarm go off, indicating an email was being composed. He knew it was either from Kadyrov or Homeland Security, because Ramadi was now dead, unless someone else was messing with Ramadi's computer. No, the composer of the email was Kadyrov. He read the computer keystrokes as Niko typed the email out. Mohtaat needed the day Kadyrov was planning to make the transfer or withdrawal of funds and the name of the bank. Kadyrov's email served as a confirmation of all the information Mohtaat needed to know. Now all he had to do was be outside the bank and wait until Kadyrov came out of the bank with the money. Mohtaat knew that Kadyrov would not transfer all of the money; he would withdraw all of it but keep some for his daily expenses and other needs. Mohtaat would follow him back to wherever he was hiding, rob him of whatever amount he had withdrawn, and then kill him. That was his game plan.

He pulled out his APK Kalashnikov automatic pistol from its hiding place and did some quick cleaning. It had been a couple of years since it was last used and he wanted to make sure all parts were in good working condition. All he could do was inspect the weapon after the cleaning because he didn't have time to go out and try it at the shooting range. It was about two years ago that he'd last gone for target practice at the target range on Dundas Street, but it was too late to go to the range right now and practice. After he finished cleaning and inspecting the weapon, Mohtaat decided to go to bed and get a full night of restful sleep. He anticipated having a busy day tomorrow.

***

Early the next morning, Niko arrived at the bank and went straight to the first available teller. He filled out an electronic transfer slip, but first he needed to know how much he had in his bank account. Niko was not going to transfer all the money to his friend in Chechnya; he would keep about seven thousand dollars for expenses and for his plane ticket to fly there. He gave the teller his account number, which she promptly entered into her computer. His account came up on the screen flagged with instructions that any activity on this account had to be discussed with one of the bank managers.

"Sir, please take a seat. Mr. Johnson, the branch manager, has to speak to you in reference to your account. I already called him, so if you'd please take a seat, he will be with you in a moment," the teller said.

This spooked Niko. Something was terribly wrong. Then he saw an individual in a blue business suit walking towards him accompanied by two security guards. He was not going to wait once he saw them coming; he made a quick break towards the doors. He ran out the doors and almost knocked down Mohtaat, who was waiting just outside the bank's doors. He got on a city bus that was just taking off on Lake Shore Boulevard West going west towards Bathurst Street. Niko, still spooked, got off the Lake Shore West bus and then got on the Bathurst Street bus going towards Koreatown. He got off on Bloor Street West and walked the rest of the way to Zarif Abdulin's residence.

Niko's running out of the bank took Mohtaat by surprise. He was unable to run after Niko because that would have raised suspicion, especially from Niko. Mohtaat decided to remain calm and wait for a second chance. Maybe the police had frozen Kadyrov's account and placed an alert on his account for any type of activity. Mohtaat thought that was the reason Kadyrov ran out of the bank. He decided to walk across the street and see if the police were going to show up. If they did, then he could be sure Kadyrov's funds had been frozen. That would be bad news for him because he wouldn't be able to rob Kadyrov of his illegal and sinful gains. Mohtaat decided that Kadyrov still had to die for accepting money to carry out a religious obligation. Receiving payment was indicative of the individual's disrespect for Islam and a deadly sin as far as Mohtaat was concerned. The sinner would have to pay with his life.

Chapter 12

Chad and Reynolds arrived that morning from Washington, D.C. They were in the Canadian police conference room continuing with the background reviews of the six Boles and Tinsel employees when the police supervisor received a call from the bank indicating that someone was attempting to make a withdrawal on Kadyrov's account. They would try to hold the person until the police could arrive.

"Agent Winters, someone is trying to withdraw money from Kadyrov's bank account! Let's go, men. They're going to try to hold the person until we get there, so let's go! Let's just hope there's no shoot-out!" yelled the police supervisor.

Reynolds and Chad stopped their review of the Boles and Tinsel employees, got in the police car with the two officers working with them on the case, and raced to the bank. The police supervisor and two other officers were in a second car. Both cars got to the bank almost at the same time, with sirens blaring and flashing lights on. When they got out of the cars, Reynolds whispered to the supervisor that he and Chad would not go in. He was going to stay close to Winters because the agent might kill Kadyrov right there on the spot.

Hearing this, the supervisor yelled out, "I want everyone to stay outside! Only Lieutenant Johnson goes in to check out the situation!"

Lieutenant Johnson went in and quickly came out, saying, "Come on in, sir. The person ran out of the bank when he was being approached by security and jumped on a city bus. He's gone, sir."

Mohtaat was standing across the street, observing everything from a non-compromising position. He heard the police supervisor turn to the black individual standing to his right and say, "Let's go inside, Agent Winters, and talk to the bank manager. Hopefully he can confirm it was Kadyrov attempting the withdrawal."

"Yes sir," replied Chad.

Mohtaat watched all the officers go inside the bank and said to himself, "So, Winters is the black individual, the infidel that al-Baghdadi wants eliminated. I don't know why everyone has failed to carry out that simple assignment." Then, an idea flashed in Mohtaat's mind. "I'm going to advise al-Baghdadi that I can carry out the assignment to eliminate the infidel where other nincompoops have failed."

He decided he'd seen enough and headed back home with the intention of sending an email to the terrorist ISIS leader advising him he was willing to undertake the mission of eliminating the American infidel—the failed mission of incompetent holy warriors.

***

Once the interview of the bank official was complete, the police supervisor and his contingent of law enforcement officers, including Chad and Reynolds, returned to the police station to continue with the investigation.

"Sir, are there any traffic cameras that we can access to check on the movements of the suspect?" asked Chad, addressing the police supervisor.

"Yes, we have security traffic cams all over town. We have one where Kadyrov supposedly got on the bus. We have cameras up and down Lake Shore Boulevard and at the intersections where the bus stops are. We can start there and see if we can spot where the suspect got off," said the police supervisor.

That same day, the police supervisor requested the footage from the cameras, starting with the one located at the Lake Shore Boulevard bus stop, camera number 9331, where Kadyrov got on. Camera 8145, at the intersection of Lake Shore and Bathurst Street West, showed him getting off and then getting on the Bathurst Street West bus. Camera 8048, located on the corner of Bathurst and Bloor, showed him getting off and walking west on Bloor Street. There was no other footage of the suspect.

"We need to canvass that neighborhood around Koreatown and see if anybody has seen the individual around that area. Who knows, we might get lucky," said the police supervisor.

***

The police supervisor set up a task force to canvass the area where they saw Kadyrov get off the bus, at the corner of Bathurst Street West and Bloor Street. The area was made up of multicultural businesses, mostly Korean, with a few apartments and houses. People of many different ethnicities resided in this particular area of Toronto. The task force spread out, visiting the business owners and managers, asking each of them if they had seen Kadyrov and showing them his picture. After getting nowhere, Chad asked the police supervisor if they could access the cameras in that area and check the footage for the past week or so.

"That's a grand idea, Agent Winters. I'll start the request right now and we'll see if we can find the individual that way. Great idea!"

Chapter 13

As soon as he arrived at his apartment, Mohtaat got on his computer and composed an email to Sheikh al-Baghdadi, the ISIS leader, that read:

"You have employed individuals in the past incapable of carrying out your demand of eliminating FBI Agent Winters. The infidel is alive and well and enjoying the unholy fruits of the Satan nation. Your last hire, Niko Adel Kadyrov, eliminated the Knights, but they were not related in any way to the infidel. Kadyrov left a trail of breadcrumbs and would have been apprehended if I had not intervened on his behalf. I have no use for such an incompetent individual so I will let him be arrested by the American authorities. He served your purpose somewhat, I suppose. I am offering you my professional services for a modest fee to finally eliminate the infidel Winters. My fee is two hundred and fifty thousand American dollars. I will do your bidding for that amount and promise you the results you wish. The elimination of FBI Agent Winters. I will not fail you. I will patiently wait for your reply." It was signed "A True Believer and a jihadist."

Finding himself short of money and knowing Kadyrov might not be able to withdraw funds from his frozen account, Mohtaat had decided to request payment for his services. Let everybody else be damned!

Al-Baghdadi received the unencrypted email and considered the message a fraud. He figured the email was from someone trying to trick him for the money. But al-Baghdadi started thinking and said to himself, "Only a few people outside of Raqqa or, for that matter, in the infidel nation know my email address. Yusuf Khalifa, Benjamin Masjid, and Kadyrov are the only ones that I sent emails to. How did this individual get my email address? Did he get it from Yusuf's computer when Yusuf was shot and killed? Or did he get it from Masjid, who was killed mysteriously? If he did not get my email from one or the other, then it's the infidel himself who sent the email, trying to trick me. Well, let me send him a reply and find out."

Chapter 14

Mooney was a street hustler and a good friend of Abdulin whenever he needed a sexual favor, though of course for money. She rang the doorbell and it was answered by Abdulin. He decided to refer Mooney to Kadyrov downstairs instead of sending her away.

His friend had not left the basement bedroom for quite a number of days now, since coming back scared from the bank. Also, Abdulin's girlfriend, Madina, had moved in with him, so he could not have sex with Mooney now. He walked her down to the basement and introduced her to Niko.

"Niko, this is Mooney, a very good friend of mine, and I thought you might enjoy her company while you stay here with us," said Zarif Abdulin.

Niko and Mooney shook hands while Zarif walked up the staircase and out of the room.

They started talking but soon Niko told Mooney he was low on funds. She got up to walk out when the idea hit Niko. Hell, use her to get my money. It would take less than thirty minutes to train her how to access his account. But, the problem was, could he trust her? What if she ran away with the money? Well, he had no money now, so what would be the difference if she ran away? No difference. So, he decided to trust her and told her to sit down while he explained what she had to do. He agreed to pay her one thousand Canadian dollars for her labor. Mooney agreed without hesitation to do it.

"Mooney, enter my account number, but before you enter the last digit of the account, hold the alt key down. Keep holding the alt key down and enter the delete key. Release the two keys and enter the following keys in sequence. This will bypass the security wall and open another window. Enter the account number again in the new window and my password. This new window will have a box where you will enter the amount of withdrawal. Enter five thousand Canadian dollars in that box. The bank's ATM machine will issue you fifty bills of one hundred dollars each. The one-hundred-dollar bill is the largest denomination the Canadian government has in circulation. The five hundred and one thousand-dollar bills were taken out of circulation sometime back due to criminal activity. Don't look up into the camera while you access the account. Walk casually away once you withdraw the money. Don't run or else your actions will raise suspicion."

"That sounds easy. What if I walk away with the money, Niko?" asked Mooney.

"Then you, Mooney Gallagher, will be out of big bucks," said Niko. "We can do it again and again and get big bucks. This is a dry run to see if my computer calculations work on the bank's computer. If it works once, we can do it again. I will pay you one thousand dollars once you get back here. If it doesn't work, then we both don't make any money."

The statement about doing it again was not true, but Niko wanted to entice her to come back with the five thousand dollars. He was hoping that by playing to her greed, she would return with the money, expecting to get more.

"I thought you said this was your account and your money, Niko."

"It is my account. But, think for a minute, how much money we can access from other accounts once I'm able to get their passwords."

This really interested Mooney and she set out to do Niko's bidding, returning in less than two hours with the five thousand Canadian dollars after encountering no problems carrying out the task. Nobody stopped her and nobody questioned her. She returned back to Zarif's residence very excited and ready to celebrate the successful mission. After she was paid her one thousand dollars and they each drank a glass of Moscato wine, Niko and Mooney continued their celebration by engaging in passionate lovemaking. This was going to be a relationship Niko wanted to fully establish; Mooney was a white Canadian girl and he was going to use her and her white privilege.

Chapter 15

The bank manager called the police supervisor as soon as he was advised by accounting that the account of Niko Adel Kadyrov had been tampered with and a total of five thousand Canadian dollars had been withdrawn by an unknown individual.

"I understood, sir, that the account had been frozen and that any activity would be noticed by your bank personnel!" replied the police supervisor very angrily.

"Yes, but in this instance, sir, the perpetrator hacked the account and withdrew the money."

"What do you mean his account was hacked? Were other accounts hacked or just his?" asked the police supervisor.

"Only his account, according to the information my accounting department has given me. We checked other accounts but it seems his was the only one hacked. Who hacked his account is the question," replied the bank manager.

"So, we don't know if Kadyrov is the one who withdrew the money. Is that what you're telling me?"

"Yes, sir, that's correct. We're now checking the video camera that's above the bank's ATM to see who the individual was," replied the bank manager.

"Okay, we'll be over at the bank in the next few minutes," said the police supervisor.

The police supervisor called Chad, Reynolds, and the two officers assigned to assist the investigation and notified them of what he'd been told by the bank manager.

"They don't know who made the withdrawal or if this was a random hack on the account. We need to get up there and get our hands around this situation," said the police supervisor.

The group of law enforcement officers got to the bank and went directly to a conference room with a television set next to the conference table. When everyone was in their seat, the bank manager turned the video on. It showed a young woman entering the account number and then other numbers in a sequence. It took her less than sixty seconds to enter the numbers on the bank's ATM. She never looked up during the whole process. She withdrew the money and quickly exited the building, again without looking up.

"That is all we have on this incident," said the bank manager to the group of officers.

"So, she did hack Kadyrov's bank account? Was she put up to it? Is this the only account that was hacked, sir?" asked Chad.

"Yes, sir. Kadyrov's account was the only one hacked."

"Well, we have to assume from this that she's an accomplice," said Chad, starting to think out loud. "But wait, are we missing something here? Or, rather, I missed something on the way. First, we have one guy we're looking for, that's Kadyrov, then the mysterious caller with the private number comes into the picture and tips off Kadyrov about the pending raid by the police. Then we have this young woman hacking his account. Is the woman working with Kadyrov, is she working by herself, or is she assisting the mysterious caller? This is getting a bit confusing, so we need to take a step back and review everything we have on this investigation. I think we'll find our answer if we first know how the spyware virus program got onto Mary's computer," said Chad, addressing Reynolds and the three Canadian officers.

"You lost me there, buddy, and most probably everyone else. What do you mean, 'We'll find the answer if we know about the virus?'" asked Reynolds. "And who's Mary? What does the spyware virus program and Mary have to do with these three individuals?"

"A lot. Mary is the DHS employee. Her computer was targeted by someone who either sent her an email with an infected message or manually loaded the spyware program onto her computer. That's how the mysterious caller was able to tip off Kadyrov that the police were on to him. I believe he was reading Mary's computer keystrokes and found out we had identified Kadyrov. If the computer was infected by an email, we'll find the infected email and follow it back to the source by its IP address. I'm going to say that someone manually loaded the spyware program on her computer and it wasn't an infected email, but we'll still keep that in mind as a possibility," replied Chad.

"Let's go back and review the Boles and Tinsel employees. We'll start there instead of getting DHS to check for an infected email if there is one. I believe our answer is in the list of employees. I think one of them manually loaded the spyware program on Mary's computer when they went through the orientation session with DHS," replied Chad.

Chad, Reynolds, and the police supervisor headed back to the police office.

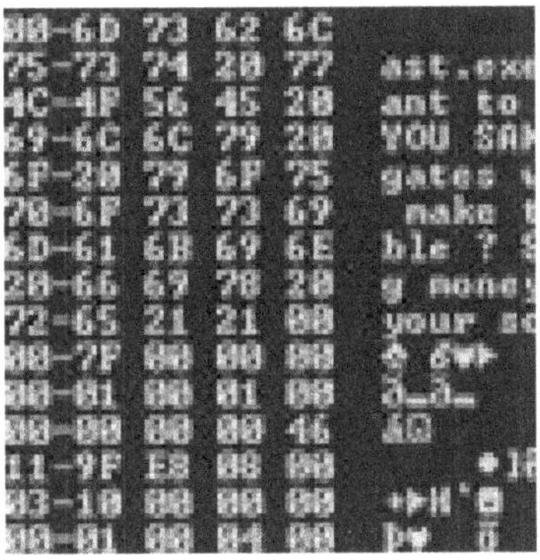

Chapter 16

Niko decided to send an encrypted email to al-Baghdadi to let him know he was going on the run. He wrote that he'd been staying with Zarif Abdulin at his house in Toronto, but that he and his friend would be leaving soon. His plan was to cross into the United States and hopefully hide in Denver, Colorado, with friends of the now-deceased Imam Masjid. Once he was situated there, he would send him an update. He closed with *insha Allah* (God willing).

The email generated an alarm on Mohtaat's laptop, advising him of an email being sent on one of the compromised computers. He quickly got up from his *toshak* and went to look at who was writing the email. It was from Niko Adel Kadyrov, the Uzbekistani.

"So, you are staying with Zarif Abdulin here in Toronto and you're going to make a run for it and hide in the Satan nation. Well, let's see if you can make it out of Canada, you worthless so-called holy warrior," Mohtaat said to himself.

As soon as he finished reading the email, Mohtaat starting searching for Abdulin's home address in the white pages online. It took Mohtaat a couple of hours before he found the address. It was near Koreatown in Toronto, about an hour's drive from his own apartment. Mohtaat decided to take his Kalashnikov pistol with the silencer to get the job done, not knowing what he might encounter. He took a taxicab from his home and had the driver drop him off two blocks from his destination. Mohtaat wanted to scout the area, first for cameras and second for police officers on duty, before going into Abdulin's house. It was almost eleven at night when he was satisfied he wasn't in any danger of being caught by a camera or police officer. No police officers were around that area and he didn't notice any street cameras. It made him very comfortable. He approached the front door of the residence very cautiously and saw the front room lights were on. Someone was up. Mohtaat rang the doorbell and Abdulin opened the front door.

"Yes, can I help you?" asked Abdulin.

"I'm looking for Brother Niko Kadyrov. He is an old acquaintance of mind," answered Mohtaat.

"Oh, where do you know him from?"

"From Uzbekistan, where we grew up."

Abdulin started doubting the stranger. Nobody knew that Niko had been staying with him. Furthermore, Niko was hiding from the authorities, and then all of a sudden, this character shows up looking for him? This sounded very suspicious, so he decided to quiz the stranger further.

"Yes, but what city?" asked Abdulin.

"You seem to doubt my sincerity, sir," replied Mohtaat, at the same time pulling out his pistol from his waistband and forcing himself into the residence. Abdulin was not expecting this quick reaction from the stranger and reacted instinctively, throwing a punch at him. Mohtaat shot Abdulin, almost at point-blank range. Madina was in the bathroom and had finished brushing her teeth when she heard the commotion coming from the front room. She came out of the bathroom, holding a glass half-full of water.

Mohtaat saw her and asked, "Where is Niko?" Instead of answering him, Madina let out a very loud scream and threw the glass she was carrying at him. Mohtaat caught the flying glass with his left hand so it wouldn't crash to the floor and make a noise and fired a shot at her to stop her from screaming any further. He placed the glass on the coffee table, reminding himself to make sure he cleaned off his fingerprints before he left the house.

After making sure both Abdulin and Madina were dead, Mohtaat searched the house. He went downstairs and checked the basement. It looked like it had been occupied but no one was there. There were no personal belongings of any kind in the closet, indicating that Niko had already skipped town. Then he heard a noise coming from the first floor; he quickly pulled out his pistol and guardedly walked up the stairs. The noise he heard was coming from the building adjacent to the house, but he was sure someone was standing just outside the door. He got spooked and decided to exit the house before it was too late. He saw a person walking towards the residence and decided to wisely walk away, going in the opposition direction. He never cleaned his prints off the water glass.

***

Niko and Mooney had left Abdulin's residence around seven in the evening that same day. Mooney had secured a small rental car at the local car rental agency using her own credit card. They loaded up Niko's few belonging at Abdulin's apartment house and then went to Mooney's apartment, which she shared with a friend, to pick up her stuff. Then they left Toronto with the intention of crossing into the United States. The Canadian border is more porous than the southern border of the United States, making it easy for anyone to cross into the United States with no major problems. Their destination was Denver, Colorado, the Mile-High City near the Rockies.

Masoud Mohtaat, using the passport with the name Alfred Robinson on it, was also on his way to Denver. He knew that Niko planned to stay with friends of Imam Benjamin Masjid. His plan was to get a place near the Muslim Center Mosque in Denver and wait for Niko to use his computer. Niko's last message to al-Baghdadi had said he would tell him where he was once he was situated in Denver. Mohtaat had all the time in the world, so waiting in the Mile-High City would not be a problem.

Chapter 17

Chad called the computer tech supervisor in the DHS office in Washington, D.C., to check Mary's computer for any sign of infected email messages, just to be sure her computer had not been infected that way. In the meantime, he and Reynolds went over the Boles and Tinsel employee list in the office of the Royal Canadian Mounted Police supervisor, checking for any clues. After a few hours of reviewing background checks on the six employees, nothing suspicious was noted on any of the employees. They were concentrating their review on Margaret Grimes. Was she the woman who withdrew the money from Kadyrov's account? Did she have the computer skills to hack the account? Just then, the police supervisor summoned everyone into his office to report the homicide of a man and a woman in the Koreatown area. Maybe the victim was Kadyrov. That was the area of Toronto where he was last seen getting off the bus.

"Gentlemen, we just got a call of a double homicide that might possibly be Kadyrov and the young lady who withdrew the money. The homicide was reported by the manager of a restaurant located next door to the residence where he found the bodies not more than five minutes ago. I already notified the medical examiner and his team, and they are on the way there. Chad, do you want to join my detectives going out there?" asked the police supervisor.

"Yes, sir. Both Reynolds and I are ready to join them."

Reynolds noticed the disappointment in Chad's face when the police supervisor said that the victim could possibly be Kadyrov.

"Are you okay, buddy?"

"Yes, I am, Reynolds."

Reynolds knew something was definitely wrong because Chad usually didn't call him by his last name. But he decided to let it go, hoping that he was just reading too much into Chad's reaction.

They arrived at the address, where two police officers stood guarding the front door of the residence, keeping the press out. First to go in was the medical examiner with his two-man medicolegal team, who had arrived minutes before everyone else. The shocked and visibly scared restaurant manager was waiting with the two officers and three news reporters outside the house. One of the detectives arriving with Chad, Reynolds, and the police supervisor took the manager aside and started interviewing him.

"I was walking towards my restaurant next door when I saw a person I didn't recognize walk out of the front door of the house. He looked around and then walked away from me, going west up that street. There's no light on that corner so I don't know where he went from there. I knocked on the door of Abdulin's residence and no one answered. The door was slightly open so I went in and that's when I saw both of them on the floor. I ran to the restaurant and called the police from there. I didn't have my cell phone on me," said the manager in a shaky voice.

"Can you describe the person you saw?" asked the interviewing detective.

"No, sir."

"But you said he was a person you didn't recognize. You saw him, but you can't describe him?"

"I didn't really see his face. He was a tall man, as tall as you. Mr. Abdulin is my height, five-feet four-inches tall. So, I knew it wasn't him," replied the manager.

"Who is Mr. Abdulin?" asked Chad.

"Zarif Abdulin is the resident of the house. He's the one that I saw on the floor."

"Who is the woman?" asked the detective.

"She's Madina, Zarif's girlfriend," replied the still-shaking manager.

Chad, Reynolds, and the police supervisor went into the house to check on the evidence being collected by the forensic team, which had arrived right after the medical examiner and his medicolegal team.

"Both individuals were shot in the face at close range. There's water spilled here on the floor in front of the woman. I don't know where the water came from," said the medical examiner.

"We found two spent shells on the floor but can't tell the type of weapon yet. We also noticed this glass on top of the coffee table that seems to have had water in it. We're checking the prints on it. Maybe the water came from the glass," said one of the forensic inspectors.

"We should have some results quickly, Agent Winters, once we get back to the office," said the other officer.

Chad was thinking that this investigation was starting to mirror the previous one, where possible witnesses and persons of interest were getting eliminated. This started to bother Chad, but he was no longer disappointed, knowing Kadyrov was not the victim of this crime. Reynolds noticed the change in Chad's disposition but didn't say anything.

"Where's the restaurant manager? I need to ask him one other question. Can someone get him for me?" asked Chad.

"He's still talking to one of the detectives outside," replied Reynolds.

"Let's go outside then," said Chad. "Was there anyone else staying with Abdulin and his girlfriend, Madina?" asked Chad, addressing the manager.

"I don't know, sir. But around seven in the evening, a man and a young woman came to the house and picked up some men's clothing, a small suitcase, and a laptop computer, and then left. They went into the house and came out in less than ten minutes. I was sitting outside the restaurant smoking a cigarette when they arrived. I don't know if they were staying with Zarif and Madina. I never saw them there," said the manager.

After hearing that the person seen leaving Zarif's residence was carrying a laptop computer, Chad turned to the police supervisor and asked, "Sir, has Ramadi's computer been analyzed?"

"I have one of my most experienced computer techs checking Ramadi's computer for email evidence right now as we speak, Agent Winters. But what does the computer have to do with this murder?" asked the police supervisor.

"We need to get back to your office and talk to your computer tech. I'll explain what my theory is once your tech checks the computer. I think I know how this character is tracking his victims," said Chad.

The four of them, Chad, Reynolds, the police supervisor, and the driver, got into the police supervisor's car and headed back to the office.

Once they were in the office, Chad went back to where the computer tech was working on Ramadi's computer and said, "Please check the computer for any type of spyware virus program and, if it is infected, see if you can determine what type of spyware program it is."

"Yes, sir, I can do that, but it's going to take some time. I'll let you know, sir, as soon as I have something," replied the computer tech.

Returning from lunch the next day, Chad, Reynolds, and the police supervisor were met at the entrance to the supervisor's office by the computer tech, who excitedly told them he was able to determine that Ramadi's computer was infected with the virus SpyMaster Keystroke Shot.

This was all the information Chad needed to connect the dots and determine that the spyware virus had been uploaded by someone on both computers, Mary's and Ramadi's.

"That's what I thought," said Chad to the police supervisor and Reynolds. "The victims that were killed were not the intended targets. I believe Niko Kadyrov was hiding in Abdulin's house and the killer tracked him there when Kadyrov used his computer. He didn't find Kadyrov there, so the killer shot both Abdulin and Madina. I am sure the person who did it is one of the Boles and Tinsel employees. They were in the DHS office in Washington, D.C., and now I'm positive one of them uploaded the spyware virus program onto Mary's computer while attending the DHS orientation session. Then they came to Toronto to do surveillance work on both Kadyrov and Ramadi. I believe that the person doing the surveillance waited until Ramadi was out of his apartment, then went in and uploaded the same spyware program on Ramadi's computer. I'm sure they did the same thing to Kadyrov's computer when Kadyrov was under surveillance as well and has been tracking both of them since then, but why? We'll tackle the 'why' question later. Let's go back and review what we have on each of the B and T employees."

Reynolds was the first to notice that Alfred Robinson had no information or records from any source prior to 2001.

"Sir, do you still have the assignment roster for the surveillance of both Kadyrov and Ramadi?" asked Chad.

"It might take me a while, but I'm sure I can come up with the rosters, Agent Winters," said the police supervisor.

"Good," replied Chad. "That will give me time to called DHS in Washington, D.C., and let them know they don't need to keep checking for infected emails on Mary's computer. We now know the spyware virus program was downloaded by one of the Boles and Tinsel employees during the orientation session. We need to find out who that person was."

The clerk was able to find the surveillance rosters in the storage warehouse located behind the police office in about two hours. After reviewing the roster and noting that Alfred Robinson had done a larger portion of the surveillance, on different days and on both Kadyrov and Ramadi, Robinson quickly became a person of interest. Chad surmised that Robinson was the person who had downloaded the spyware on Mary's and Ramadi's computer. He was sure he had done the same to Kadyrov's computer.

"Sir, can we send a police officer to Robinson's address and bring him in for questioning? If he refuses, we can get a warrant for his arrest as a suspect in the murders of Zarif and Madina," said Chad.

"I'll send two police officers to that address right now, Agent Winters," replied the police supervisor.

About thirty minutes later, one of the police officers called saying the address was bogus; there was no such number. They had even reversed the three numbers and checked those addresses but had had no luck.

"I think Robinson is our man," said Chad. "Can we put out an APB, sir?"

"I will do it right now, Agent Winters."

An All-Points Bulletin was put out but nothing materialized. Mohtaat, traveling as Alfred Robinson, had already crossed into the United States and was on his way to Denver, Colorado.

***

The Canadian police lab technician came back with the prints off the glass. One set of prints belonged to Madina Socii, Zarif Abdulin's girlfriend, who had a long record of prostitution arrests in Toronto and in other parts of Canada. The second set of prints belonged to a person by the name of Masoud Mohtaat.

"Now who in the hell is this Masoud Moh … whatever his name is and how did he get into the picture? Who is he?" asked Reynolds to whoever could answer.

Everybody in the room was non-responsive, except Chad.

"He's Alfred Robinson, also known as Masoud Mohtaat," said Chad. "I recalled the name Mohtaat because he's on Interpol's wanted list. Interpol is looking for him for extortion and other crimes allegedly committed in Europe."

"Agent Winters is correct," said the lab technician. "I ran the prints through all available databases and Interpol responded after they ran the prints with the name of Masoud Mohtaat. He's considered extremely dangerous and caution should be exercised when encountering this individual according to the Interpol bulletin they sent. I made a copy of the bulletin for each of you."

"Now that we know this individual is a suspect in the murders of Zarif and Medina, let's issue an arrest warrant, sir. Also, let's put out a bulletin under both names in all of the entry points to the United States and check if this person has crossed the border," said Chad, addressing the police supervisor.

"I'll do that immediately, Agent Winters. We won't rest until we capture this bastard," replied the police supervisor.

Less than two hours later, the police supervisor got a call from the supervisor at one of the border entry/exit points, informing them that the suspect had crossed into the United States at the Peace Bridge into

Buffalo, New York, two days before. He had crossed under the name of Alfred Robinson.

Now they knew that the suspect had crossed into the United States and was traveling under Robinson's name, but what was his destination? If he was following Kadyrov, did that meant that Kadyrov had also crossed into the United States? Was the girl seen leaving Zarif Abdulin's house by the restaurant manager with Kadyrov? Was Masoud Mohtaat after Kadyrov to kill him? If he was, then Chad had to find Kadyrov before that happened. He couldn't let someone else have the pleasure of killing Kadyrov. That job was all his and only his, and no one was going to deny him what was rightfully his. He decided to request the same information from the entry/exit points on Kadyrov, but after an intensive search of the crossing records at all entry/exit points by Canadian immigration personnel, no information was found about Kadyrov crossing at any of them.

Chapter 18

Kadyrov and Mooney drove to the Niagara Glen Nature Reserve, which was approximately eighty miles from Toronto, and spent the night at a small motel not far from the reserve.

"Niko, I have never been this happy before," said Mooney. "I now know that I've never been in love before because this feeling I have for you is beyond reproach."

"Mooney, honey, I feel the same way about you. Too bad we didn't meet before all of this. You would have made a big difference in the decisions I've made recently. Look what it has got me, rather ... us into."

Kadyrov knew the FBI was looking for him, so he was sure all the entry points to the United States had been alerted. They scouted the Niagara River area the next morning at the reserve, checking for the narrowest part of the river, and then went back to the city of Niagara Falls, Canada, where they were staying. Niko purchased two large backpacks and a two-person Maxim inflatable boat kit with a foot-operated air pump at one of the local sporting goods stores.

Later that afternoon, they parked the rental car in the reserve's parking lot and set out with their backpacks, with Kadyrov carrying a second large leather bag on his shoulder. They started walking on the trail to the area they'd scouted earlier that morning. They traveled through the forested area of the reserve, staying away from the hiking routes and hikers. They reached the designated area they'd scouted and Kadyrov inflated the rubber raft with the foot pump. They loaded their few personal belongings into the inflated boat and got in. They took one oar each and started guiding the raft towards the US side of the river. The current was not too strong and they reached the other side with no major problems. Kadyrov unloaded the rubber boat, took the air out, and discarded it behind some very large boulders in Devil's Hole State Park, on the American side.

They walked, as hikers, with their backpacks to Highway 61, also known as Hyde Park Boulevard; there they got a ride with a middle-aged married couple going up Highway 62. When they reached US Highway 190, Mooney and Niko got out. They eventually caught their next ride with a young couple going to Buffalo, New York, their destination. Once they reached Buffalo, they used Mooney's credit card to rent a motel room for the night.

The next morning, Mooney rented another car and they set out for Denver, Colorado, over fifteen hundred miles away. The distance didn't bother Niko or Mooney; they were in love and expressed it all the way to Denver, making love every place they stayed. Niko knew they were safe from the authorities because they would be looking only for him in Toronto, not knowing that he and Mooney were already in the United States and on their way to the Mile-High City, *alhamdulillah* (thanks be to Allah).

***

Masoud Mohtaat arrived in Denver way before Kadyrov and Mooney. He found a small hotel with Wi-Fi not far from the mosque and waited for Kadyrov to send the email he'd promised al-Baghdadi, letting him know where he was. Mohtaat traveled to and from the mosque, going on different streets and checking out hotels and motels in the area where Kadyrov might try to hide once he arrived in Denver. Mohtaat was very confident that no one knew of him, and not wiping his fingerprints off the glass he left behind at Zarif's house didn't bother him either. Anyway, there were no records of his fingerprints in Canada, so why worry? He had his computer set up in his hotel room, so he just waited for the computer alarm to go off.

He was watching the Alt-right News Channel when the Washington, D.C., news anchor had FBI Agent Chad Winters live on the air with the announcement that Masoud Mohtaat, also known as

Alfred Robinson, was a suspect in the murder of two Canadians, Zarif Abdulin and his girlfriend, Madina Socii. Chad had used this venue to see if he could scare Mohtaat and keep him away from Kadyrov. If anyone was going to kill Kadyrov, it was going to be him. Chad mentioned in the news announcement that the victims had been murdered in Toronto, Canada, and the suspect was believed to have crossed into the United States.

Mohtaat was shocked when he saw the news. He had registered using the name Alfred Robinson, so he knew the hotel clerk would be calling the police right away, if he hadn't called them already. He decided to quickly gather his belongings, including his computer, and go somewhere else and register under a different name.

He had stolen fellow employee Abel Suttles' driver's license and one of his credit cards when they both worked with Boles and Tinsel, so he could use that license for identification purposes. He'd had a friend back in Toronto replace Suttles' picture with his own on the driver's license. He didn't need a credit card to get a hotel room; he would use the stolen credit card only in a dire situation. All he'd had to do was give the desk clerk a couple of twenties to allow him to register and pay cash up front without any questions asked. The authorities didn't have his picture, so that would help, but he couldn't stay at this hotel.

He decided to leave the rental car in the hotel's parking lot, walk three blocks, grab a taxi, and go to another hotel across town. He had to rethink his strategy now that the FBI had identified him. Mohtaat made up his mind that he had to eliminate Agent Winters, even if he wasn't paid by al-Baghdadi.

***

Kadyrov and Mooney arrived in Denver and checked into a hotel close to the mosque under Mooney's name. They were watching a comedy show on television when it was interrupted by the breaking news announcing the murders of Zarif and Madina.

"My lord! Who would have done it? And it was committed the same night we left their house! What have you done, Niko? Who is after you?" asked Mooney, scared.

"I don't know, Mooney! But we're safe here. Nobody knows we crossed the border because we didn't go through the border crossing. That's why we did what we did, Mooney. We're safe here," said Niko, trying to reassure Mooney, though he himself was not too sure they were safe.

مؤسسة الزوراء للإنتاج الإعلامي

المنبر الاعلامي الجهادي

Chapter 19

Chad and Reynolds returned to Washington, D.C., when Chad determined that Kadyrov had, somehow or other, managed to cross the international border into the United States without being recorded. He was positive of that. That was the reason why Masoud Mohtaat also crossed into the United States. Nobody knew where he was going except Mohtaat himself.

Chad made up his mind he had to find Kadyrov before Mohtaat, or else Kadyrov was a dead man. He wanted to capture Kadyrov alive to question him about who put him up to killing the Knights. Chad couldn't rest until he knew the answer. Then, he was going to kill Kadyrov. There was no question about that.

The FBI hotline got a call from the Denver police department that the suspect, Masoud Mohtaat, had been staying for the past three days in the Sunrise Hotel, located in the southern outskirts of Denver. The Denver police had gone to the hotel, but the room was vacant. The suspect's rental car was still in the hotel's parking garage. That was all the information Chad needed to determine that Mohtaat, and possibly Kadyrov, were in Denver.

Chad and Reynolds flew that same evening from Dulles International Airport to Denver International, arriving late at night. They went directly to a hotel in Aurora, Colorado, ready to start looking for Mohtaat early the following day. Was Kadyrov also in Denver? Chad thought he was, or else Mohtaat would not have made the trip there from Toronto. Mohtaat was going to lead them to Kadyrov and that was an excellent reason for Chad to find him.

***

Despite what he told Mooney, Niko was scared that two individuals were now looking for him. He knew one was Winters, the FBI special agent, but he had no idea who the second individual was. Was it the same person who called him a few weeks ago, telling him to get out of Toronto because Winters was looking for him? Was he the one that killed Ramadi, Zarif, and Madina? No. It couldn't be the same individual. The unknown caller called him to warn him about Winters, so he couldn't be the same person who was after him. The unknown caller said he was a friend. But why was this other unknown individual after him? Regardless, not knowing who the individual or individuals were was really scaring him.

How could he protect himself from this killer when he didn't know who he was? Where could he run to? But wait. He was getting uptight for nothing. Nobody knew he had crossed the border, not even the unknown caller or the killer. The killer must have followed him to Zarif's house and, when he didn't find him there, killed Zarif and Madina. He didn't tell Zarif where he was going, so he was safe here in Denver. No sense getting all excited over nothing.

Niko decided to send an encrypted email to al-Baghdadi to let him know he was safe and had arrived in Denver. He needed money, because he was unable to withdraw the funds from his bank account. Niko knew that Raqqa, the capital of the caliphate of the Islamic State in Syria, had fallen, so he was not sure if al-Baghdadi would be able to deliver on his request. He decided to send the same email to Maulana Masood Azhar, the leader of the terrorist group Jaish-e-Mohammed in Pakistan, hoping that one or the other would answer. He knew that Azhar had several relatives in Denver who used to be friends of the now-deceased Imam Masjid. Maybe he would get the home address of at least one relative of Azhar here in Denver. Then he would be able to have the funds deposited into their account. Most importantly, he might be able to seek refuge and safety in their home.

He wrote in his email that he was staying temporarily in a motel near the Denver Muslim Center Mosque but had no funds to continue with the holy missions. He needed money and was hoping to get the name of a relative of Azhar for two reasons: to deposit the funds into their bank account and also to seek safety in their residence from Winters.

After two days, Niko received a response, but not from al-Baghdadi. The email response was from Azhar, telling him he had a nephew named Rashid Binarji, who went under that name there in Denver. He had become an American citizen when he immigrated to the United States as a refugee. He did not have an address, but he was a regular attendee at the Denver Muslim Center Mosque.

"I am sure you will find him there, Brother Kadyrov. I cannot send you any funds, but I am positive you will find safe refuge in his residence, though I don't have his address. I recommend you go to the Denver mosque for prayer services and ask for him there. I am sending a copy of this email to Rashid so he can expect you. *Allah yusallmak* (May God protect you)."

***

Mohtaat read the email and decided to take a ride to the mosque. He rented another car from a small car rental agency located in a neighborhood business strip on East Colfax Avenue and East 6th Avenue in Aurora, using the stolen credit card. He knew now that Niko had no money on him, but he was still going to kill him for his disservice and disrespect to Islam. He knew the Isha prayer, the last of the five daily prayers, was held at eight thirty-one p.m. The Isha prayer is recited when darkness falls. It was still light outside, enabling Mohtaat to recon the mosque parking lot and the surrounding streets to see if he noticed anything suspicious. He parked his car in the parking lot of a convenience store across the street from the mosque, went inside the store, bought a soda, a newspaper, and some snacks, and then sat in his car until he saw Kadyrov and a young woman get out of a small car and enter the mosque.

"Hell," said Mohtaat, "I have to kill both or else the woman will be a witness. I can't let that happen."

Mohtaat waited until the prayer service was over and the worshippers were leaving the mosque. Then he saw Kadyrov and the girl walking to their car.

She was walking behind Niko when he stopped to open the passenger door so she could get in. Mohtaat got out of his car with his gun and walked across the street near the parking lot. He had taken the silencer off his weapon. Mohtaat took aim at Kadyrov's back, but at the same time Mooney swung Niko around quickly, so she was now standing in front of him, and said, "I've never been this happy before." She was shot in the head.

Niko was holding her as she said, lovingly, "I love you, Niko," and died. Scared, Niko dropped her limp body onto the pavement of the parking lot and ran in the opposite direction from where the shot had come from. Other worshippers ran to Mooney's side to help. Then Niko heard more shots and saw some of the people who had run to help Mooney fall down after getting shot too. Mohtaat decided to shoot some of the bystanders to make it look like another of the regular and recurring mass shootings in the United States.

Mohtaat said to himself, "The stupid Americans should know by now that radical Muslims don't have to come to the United States to kill Americans. Eventually, the gun lobby will have all the crazy but in-good-standing Americans armed with AR-15s, and they will continue the American sport of killing their own."

Once he emptied the fifteen rounds, Mohtaat ran to his car and drove in the opposite direction, knowing that the police would be arriving any minute now. He drove back to the hotel where he was staying, elated that he had killed some worshippers, *alhamdulillah* (thanks be to Allah).

***

Niko did not have that much money on him, since he had given Mooney fifteen hundred dollars for a money order to pay her credit card balance. He had enough money to get a taxi, which he did, after running about six blocks from the mosque. He had Rashid Binarji's home address after acquiring it from Rashid when he met him outside the mosque before the prayer service. He hoped that nothing had happened to Rashid or his wife, who were at the mosque when the shooting started. Niko waited outside Binarji's house, hiding behind some bushes, until Rashid and his wife got home. He was relieved when he saw both getting out of their car. The three of them went into the house and quickly decided that Niko would not be going anywhere if he was going to stay with them. Going out of the house would endanger both husband and wife.

"Niko, if you're going to stay with us, you can't be going out in the open. We would also be in danger," said Rashid.

Niko agreed but his problem now was that he no longer had his laptop computer to communicate with the outside world, especially al-Baghdadi or Azhar. He was alive, though, and had to make the best of it. Like it or not, Niko had no other choice.

***

The FBI quickly got involved in the investigation because the mass shooting had all the signs of a hate crime, since it had taken place at a mosque. Four worshippers had been killed and seven others were wounded. One of the individuals killed was a young Canadian by the name of Mooney Gallagher, whose last known address was in Koreatown in Toronto.

"This was not a hate crime or a mass shooting," said Chad. "You can call it a mass shooting, but I believe it was made to look like a mass shooting to hide the real target, Niko Adel Kadyrov. I am sure Ms. Gallagher is the person who withdrew the money from Niko's account in Toronto. Let's send a picture of Miss Gallagher to the Canadian police for comparison with the person on the bank's ATM video. I'll bet you we'll get a match. But where did Niko go? He left Gallagher's rental car there. Did someone pick him up or did he get a taxi? Let's run that past the taxicab companies and ask if any of their taxis picked up a passenger at the mosque or not far from the mosque around ten that night. The shooter at the mosque was Masoud Mohtaat and that's why he crossed into the United States, to kill Kadyrov. The question is, why does he want Kadyrov dead? We've got to find Kadyrov before Mohtaat does."

***

Masoud Mohtaat got back to his hotel room very upset that he had failed. "I had a clear shot if that stupid woman hadn't got in the way. I would have already completed my holy mission if she hadn't been there. But I'm sure I'll have another opportunity to complete my mission, *insha Allah* (God willing)."

أعماق
الإخبارية

Chapter 20

Chad and Reynolds went to the morgue the following morning to get personal information on Ms. Mooney Gallagher. They went through her purse, which had her Canadian driver's license, four credit cards, a hotel key, and some wallet-size family pictures. The hotel key had the name and address of the hotel, so they went there with an arrest warrant for Niko Kadyrov and a police squad in case he was still in the hotel room. Reynolds showed the arrest warrant to the night manager who was on duty, but they were told the room had been cleaned less than an hour ago and no one was in the room. The night manager told them that the bed had not been slept in, but they were still considered occupants of the hotel, having paid up for one more week.

The manager was advised that Ms. Gallagher had been shot the night before and that the police were looking for Mr. Kadyrov. He was not a suspect, but they wanted to question him about the shooting. They secured the room key and went into the room to check for any evidence they could find. Mooney's and Niko's clothes were still in the closet and personal items were in the drawers. Niko's laptop was found on top of a small desk.

"I think we hit the jackpot," said Chad. "We'll use Niko's laptop to capture Mohtaat."

"I don't get it," said Reynolds. "How are we going to do that?"

"Masoud Mohtaat downloaded the spyware virus onto Mary's computer at the headquarters of Homeland Security in Washington, D.C., then Ramadi's computer at his apartment in Toronto, and I'm sure he did the same to Niko's computer while doing surveillance work for the

Canadian police. That's how Mohtaat has been tracking Niko. Here's how we're going to lure him to a place where we'll be waiting for him." Chad explained his plan to Reynolds and then set out to recon the place they wanted to lure Mohtaat to.

***

The alarm on Mohtaat's computer went off, notifying him of an outgoing email. The composer of the email was Niko and the email was going to al-Baghdadi.

It said, "I had to move to a different hotel because of a shooting. I'm staying at the Rainbow Circle Motel in Aurora, Colorado. I will give you more details later. Kadyrov."

Mohtaat read the email but was suspicious because of its brevity.

"Why isn't he asking for money? He could not withdraw or transfer the funds. Well, I shouldn't be worried about that. Kadyrov is running scared and I'm sure that's the reason for the shortness of the message," Mohtaat said to himself.

This was the opportunity he was waiting for, to complete his personal holy mission on Kadyrov for his faithlessness. He pulled the Kalashnikov pistol from its hiding place and loaded it with double-stack magazines. Then he screwed on the silencer and was ready to go. He looked up the address of the Rainbow Circle Motel and then set out to check out the area. He noticed the motel was about twelve miles from his; it would take him about twenty to thirty minutes to get there, due to construction on some of the streets. He was ready to complete his holy mission, *alhamdulillah* (praise be to Allah).

***

Chad and Reynolds had selected this particular motel because of its isolation from the busy business area and because the motel had only six rooms. The isolation of the motel and its small size was ideal for safety purposes in case of a shoot-out. They knew that Mohtaat was a dangerous individual and had proven that more than once. They showed their FBI credentials to the motel owner and explained what their purpose was. The motel owner was hesitant at first, but when they explained to him that the target was the shooter from the Denver mosque, he changed his mind, though he still hadn't bought into the FBI's plan.

"Look, we need all six rooms for our operation. We know that this type of motel is used for sex purposes, so we want to rent all six rooms for our mission. We don't want you to rent any rooms while we're here, okay? We're not here to close your operation because of the nature of your business, though we could do that very quickly. Do you understand?"

"Yes, sir, I do. And I will not rent any rooms while you carry out your operation," replied the motel owner.

"We really appreciate you working with us to bring this individual to justice. Well, there is one other thing," said Chad. "The suspect might call you to make sure a person by the name of Niko Adel Kadyrov is in one of the rooms. If he calls, you tell him, 'Yes, he's in his room.' Then follow up by asking him if he wants you to ring his room. If he says 'yes,' you ring the room where I will be and I'll answer the call. I'll be in the middle room, which is room 102. I don't think he'll do that, but you never know, so we have to plan for any contingency."

"I'll be more than glad to do what you ask, Agent Winters," replied the motel owner.

After he finished talking to the motel owner, Chad went to his car and retrieved Niko's computer. Then he went into room 102 and sent out the fake email, hoping he was right that the computer was how Mohtaat was tracking Kadyrov and that he would read it. Chad then called the FBI office in Denver and told the agent in the office to have seven male and three female agents near the motel. They were to pair up with one male agent each, drive to the motel office a pair at a time, pretend to register, and then go to one of the rooms they would be assigned to. Chad advised the agent in the office to have all of the agents wear their Kevlar flak vests for protection. The additional agents were to serve as backup in case they were needed.

He and Reynolds set up shop in room 102 and assigned one officer to room 101 and the other to room 103. The two other officers drove the cars they had used to get to the motel back to a predetermined staging area, but they left one behind just in case it was needed in a dire emergency. All cars were unmarked and the two officers wore civilian clothes, like the others in the rooms next to Chad and Reynolds.

It was around seven p.m. when Chad and Reynolds noticed a mid-size car drive around the block three times. Chad also got a call from one of the officers in the staging area notifying him that there was a vehicle going around the motel looking very suspicious. They determined it was the same vehicle Chad and Reynolds had noticed, so everyone was put on alert. The suspicious car parked at the end of the street, not far from the motel, with a full view of the manager's office in front and stayed there.

Chad put his plan in motion. He called the female agents and their partners and asked them to drive up one at a time in ten-minute increments, register, and take their positions in their assigned rooms. Two of the female/male teams had registered when Chad called the agent in room 101 and told him to come out without a shirt, smoke a cigarette outside, and then go back into his room after five minutes. The last team showed up and did the same, registered and went to their assigned room.

The suspicious car was still parked in the same location. Around seven forty p.m. the person inside the car got out and slowly made his way towards the motel, trying to stay away, as much as possible, from the lighted areas. The person was moving towards rooms 102 and 103. It was the wrong time for a new motel customer to arrive with a date, but as the person walked closer to room 102, the potential customer parked his car in front of the manager's office. The man and his date were going to be caught in the crossfire, if there was any, so Chad and Reynolds decided to make their move prematurely.

They popped out of the room and identified themselves, yelling "FBI! Get on the ground!" But instead of following the agents' orders, Mohtaat yelled, "*Allahu akbar!*" (God is great) and started shooting. The first-person hit was the surprised motel customer who had just arrived. His date didn't wait to find out what was going on. She got out of the car and sprinted across the parking lot and down the street, never to be seen again. Mohtaat started shooting at Chad and Reynolds, hitting Reynolds in the chest. By then, all of the other officers had come out of their rooms and started shooting at Mohtaat. Mohtaat shot one other officer before he was killed. All of the officers, including Chad and Reynolds, were wearing Kevlar flak vests, but the bullet had penetrated Reynolds' vest.

"Two officers down! Send EMS to Rainbow Circle Motel. One civilian also shot plus the target. Send four ambulances to same address!" yelled Chad into his cell phone. He then went to where Mohtaat was lying and checked him out. He had taken three shots, all to his chest. He was dead as far as Chad could tell. The civilian had been lucky. He'd been shot in his right shoulder and was taken in one of the ambulances to the hospital. Chad got into the second ambulance with the wounded Reynolds and accompanied him to the hospital. The third ambulance took the other officer, who had been shot in the ankle, to the hospital, and the last ambulance took Mohtaat's body to the morgue. He was pronounced dead upon arrival by the medical examiner.

"Please, God, don't let him die!" said Chad looking at Reynolds with tears welling in his eyes. "Tom is like a brother to me, so don't take him away! Please, God, he's all I have. He's like a relative to me."

A team of doctors was waiting at the entrance of the emergency room to provide immediate medical assistance. Reynolds was quickly examined and taken to surgery, due to the nature of the wound. The doctors told all of the officers coming in with Reynolds, including Chad, to wait in the visitors' waiting room. After almost two hours of waiting, Chad and the police chief were the only ones in the waiting room when the attending physician came in to let them know Reynolds was going to make it.

"I've got good news and bad news, sirs," said the attending physician.

"I've heard that cliché many, many times in the past, Doctor. Let's go with the good news first."

"Good news is that Agent Reynolds will recover. The bad news is that it looks like he's lost the use of his right arm. Agent Reynolds took one shot in the chest and he's alive because of the Kevlar vest. The second shot hit him in the right shoulder, tearing all of the muscle tissue and nerves. The bullet almost took his arm off. I would recommend he retire from the FBI, but that will be up to him," said the doctor.

"Can I see him now?" asked Chad.

"Yes, you can, but only for a few minutes. He's out, so you won't be able to talk to him."

"Thank you, Doctor," replied Chad and left to go visit his buddy.

Chapter 21

Niko, Rashid, and his wife had already gone to bed, so it wasn't until the following morning that they learned the mosque shooter had been killed by agents from the FBI with assistance from the local police department. The news anchor identified the shooter as Masoud Mohtaat, also known as Alfred Robinson and Abel Suttles, from Toronto. Still unknown was the motive for the mass shooting in which four worshippers were killed and seven more injured. The investigation by the FBI was still ongoing.

"So, this person by the name of Mohtaat is the killer of Ramadi, Zarif, Madina, and now Mooney. But why did he want to kill me?" Niko asked Rashid, knowing that Rashid would not be able to answer his question.

"Niko, you know you cannot stay with us for a long period of time. You need to leave and the sooner you leave, the better for us. I'll be paid this coming Friday and I can give you some money for you to leave. Both Lillia and I plan to live in peace here in the United States, free from the terror that is going on all over the Middle East, especially in Afghanistan, where Lillia is from. We are trying very hard, Niko, to be accepted here as full-fledged Americans. As you can see, Lillia does not wear a burqa since we became US citizens. Oh, by the way, Lillia is two months pregnant, so we'll be expecting our first baby soon. I think you understand our situation, Niko. You can get a ticket for the Greyhound bus and you don't have to show identification. All you have to do is decide where you want to go within the United States to hide. When you decide, and I hope you decide by this Friday, we will take you to the bus terminal," said Rashid.

Niko had no other choice but to accept their offer of assistance and leave their home. The question was, where would he go? After thinking about it for a few hours, Niko decided he should go to New York City. The terror group Jaish-e-Mohammed had, at one time, an active cell there, until it was busted by the FBI a few years ago. He was sure there were still some sympathizers who would provide him shelter. That was the only option he had.

"I've decided to take your offer of assistance and leave your residence this coming Friday. If you can take me to the bus station on Saturday, I will be most grateful," said Niko to Rashid.

"Where will you be going, Niko?" asked Rashid.

Niko knew where he was going but he wasn't going to tell Rashid, for his own safety and security. The truth was, he didn't trust Rashid.

"I don't really know where I'm going, but I'll decide once I get to the bus terminal. If you could drop me off around ten thirty in the morning, I will be very grateful," replied Niko.

Rashid got paid that Friday and gave Niko three hundred dollars from his salary. The next morning, Rashid and Lillia took Niko to the bus terminal and dropped him off at exactly ten thirty as requested. They left Niko there and returned to their home. Rashid then called the Denver FBI office located on East 36th and asked who was in charge of the mass shooting investigation.

The secretary gave the caller the name of the person in charge of the investigation and transferred the call directly to Agent Winters.

"Agent Winters, I would like to remain anonymous, but I have information that you might need on Niko Adel Kadyrov," Rashid said. "My wife and I didn't know the FBI was looking for him and, after the mosque shooting, he showed up at our house. We met during prayer service at the mosque and my wife and I were going home when the shooting occurred. We heard the shots and quickly got into our car and went home. Niko showed up later that night at our house and told us that his girlfriend, Mooney Gallagher, had been shot. He claimed he didn't know who shot Mooney, but he was scared and asked if he could stay with us. We told him 'yes' and this morning, we took him to the Greyhound Bus Terminal."

"Why didn't you call earlier? The shooting took place five days ago," said Chad.

"You have to understand, Agent Winters, both my wife and I were afraid of Niko."

Knowing that Niko had murdered the Knights, and the way he murdered them, Winters believed the caller.

"Did he tell you where he was going?"

"No, sir, Agent Winters. But the next bus out of Denver, at ten forty-five, was going to New York City. We dropped him off this morning at ten thirty, as I said before. I believe that's where Niko is going, sir."

"If he's going to New York City, who would be his contact person there, do you know?"

"No, sir, Agent Winters, I don't. If I knew, I would tell you, sir," said Rashid sincerely.

"Okay, thank you for the information, and if you think of anything else that might be helpful, please call me directly at this number."

"I definitely will, Agent Winters, and thank you for being so nice," said Rashid, hanging up.

"Nice, my ass. Wait till I have my hands on that son-o-bitch, bastard Kadyrov. That's when you'll see my kindness," said Chad to himself.

"Okay, guys. I need two of you to go with me to the bus terminal and then from there to the airport. I need someone to requisition a chopper with a pilot and the three of us will go on the chopper to intercept the bus at one of its scheduled stops. I don't believe this guy is armed, but we can't take a chance. Take your weapons and your Kevlar vests. We're taking off in ten minutes. Any questions?"

"None. We're ready to rock and roll, Agent Winters, oor-ah!" yelled one of the agents, a US Marine retiree.

***

Chad and the two FBI agents went to the bus terminal with a picture of Kadyrov to verify if he'd got on the bus going to New York

City. They were told yes, "the person with the funny smile" was on the bus going to New York City.

"Yes, Agent Winters, the bus is on its way to New York and that person is on the bus. I remember him because of his funny smile. The first stop on the route will be Kearney, Nebraska. The bus should be arriving there by three forty-five," said the ticket agent at the terminal.

"Thank you for the information, Mr. Cruz. You've been very helpful," said Chad to the agent, reading the agent's name off the name tag and moving away from the counter so he could talk freely with the two FBI agents.

"Guys, it's going on twelve noon, giving us three hours plus to get there by chopper. Let's head out to the airport. Lisa called and said the pilot with the chopper is ready to take off as soon as we get there. Let's move!" said Chad.

Chad and the two other agents arrived at a private section of the Denver International Airport where the pilot was waiting for them with a Bell 206 JetRanger Helicopter.

"What's your destination, Agent Winters?" asked the pilot.

"Kearney, Nebraska, sir," replied Chad.

"I can get you there in two hours, Agent Winters," said the pilot. "But I'll have to land in the Kearney Regional Airport and you'll have to take a car to the city, which is five miles from the airport."

"Thanks for the heads-up. I need to call Lisa at the office and have her call that airport and get them to have a car ready for us when we get there," said Chad.

The pilot got them to the airport by two fifty p.m. and by three p.m. the three agents were on the way to the Kearney stop, the first stop on the bus route.

They got to the Kearney stop a good thirty minutes ahead of the bus. Chad and the two agents agreed that he would stay inside the building while the two agents would approach Kadyrov and take him down as soon as he stepped off the bus, if he got off the bus. If he didn't get off, the agents would board as new passengers and apprehend him inside the bus. They weren't going to identify themselves as FBI agents until after Kadyrov was taken down physically, inside or outside the bus. It sounded like a good plan and the three hoped it would be executed as planned.

They saw the bus coming into the parking lot of the gas station. The two FBI agents went out, one at a time, and took positions opposite each other outside the gas station that doubled as the bus stop. The two agents blended in as regular customers among the gas station/bus stop crowd. They waited, and when they saw the passengers getting off, walked with others as if to greet relatives or friends who were getting off the bus.

Then Kadyrov got off. One of the agents got behind him and the other approached him from the front. Kadyrov saw the person approaching him and quickly figured it was the police. He turned to run but the agent behind him grabbed him and got him down to the ground. The second agent was on him almost at the same time while Winters came running from inside the gas station, flashing his FBI badge and saying, "We are FBI agents! Please step away and continue on your way! Everything is under control here!"

The two agents had already cuffed Kadyrov, who was still on the ground. Kadyrov saw Winters running from inside the gas station and started shaking violently. He looked extremely agitated when Winters got close to him, then went into what looked like a convulsion.

"Oh no, asshole, you're not dying on me! I haven't started with you yet!" yelled Chad so loud that everyone heard, but he didn't give a damn who was around him.

He grabbed Kadyrov by the throat and raised him about one foot off the ground. All the people stopped and noticed what the FBI agent was doing.

"Agent Winters, let's get Kadyrov in the car away from the crowd!" called out one of the agents.

Chad released him, and the other two agents picked Kadyrov up by the arms and dragged him to the car.

"Let's put him in the chopper and take him back with us to Denver. We'll interrogate him there in the office," said Chad.

"Don't you think we should take him to a hospital first, Agent Winters?" asked one of the agents.

"Hell no! I want to know who ordered him to murder my fiancée's parents. We'll take him to the hospital after he tells me, not before!" said Chad rather angrily.

"What if he dies, Agent Winters? Then what?"

"Not your concern, agent. This is on me and I will take full responsibility for whatever happens to this bastard," replied Chad.

They drove to the Regional Airport at Kearney, returned the car to a driver waiting for them next to the chopper, got Kadyrov into the helicopter, and flew back to Denver. Chad was thinking about what to do to Kadyrov to get him to talk. Hold him by the feet while the chopper was in the air? No. He had other plans and was ready to seek his revenge, without remorse, on Niko Adel Kadyrov, the terrorist he hated the most for killing the elderly Knights.

Chapter 22

They reached the Denver International Airport and then drove back to the FBI office, where Kadyrov was taken to the infirmary, located in the basement of the building, and given a shot to sedate him after he was examined by a physician.

"He'll be okay, Agent Winters. He was suffering what looked like a touch of excited delirium. This is something that happens to individuals when they're in acute distress or see something they didn't expect to see and it overwhelms them. He'll be okay, Agent Winters," said the attending physician.

"Thank you, Doctor. I would like to question him as soon as possible. Will you please let me know when I'll be able to do that, Doctor?"

"Of course, Agent Winters. Give him a couple hours of rest and then you can question him at length," said the doctor.

"Thank you, Doctor," said Chad and he went up to the second floor, where his temporary office was located. He got to his desk and looked in the drawer for something sharp. He found a small letter opener and put it in his pocket. "That will do for now," he said to himself.

Two hours later, Chad was downstairs with Kadyrov in the infirmary. He was still in handcuffs, but now each hand was cuffed to the side of the metal bed. Chad dismissed the security guard who was guarding Kadyrov, telling him, "I'm going to question the detainee, so take a break and be back in thirty minutes."

"Yes, Agent Winters."

Chad grabbed a chair, sat in front of Niko, and said, "Hello, Niko. You know who I am?"

Niko did not say a word but nodded his head slowly, with fear showing in his eyes.

"I want you to tell me who directed you to kill the Knights in Harker Heights, Texas," said Chad in a very calm voice.

"You go to hell!" answered Niko.

"Niko, that's the wrong answer. I'm trying my best to be nice to you, so again, who gave you your orders?"

This time, Niko didn't answer but rather spit at Winters. Oops, he shouldn't have done that. Winters got up from his chair and punched Niko in the face as hard as he could. Then he went to the door and locked it. He took a roll of gauze and a roll of tape from the medicine cabinet. He used the tape to tie Kadyrov's ankles to the sides of the metal bed. Then he said, "I will ask you one more time. Who gave you your orders, Niko?" Niko didn't answer. Chad took the gauze, placed it tightly over Niko's mouth, then went around Niko's head with the tape to secure it. Next, he took the letter opener he had in his pocket and placed it under Niko's fingernail. He pushed the letter opener under the fingernail until the nail came off.

"First, I'm going to pull all of your fingernails out, one by one, and then will ask you again, Niko."

Niko was saying, "No, no," and even with the gauze and tape over his mouth, Chad could understand what he was trying to communicate. Chad pulled out Niko's second nail while Niko yelled, moved, and wiggled to no avail. Chad pulled out the third nail and was working on the fourth when Niko said, "Al-Baghdadi! Al-Baghdadi!"

Chad stopped and pulled the gauze and tape off Niko's mouth. "It was al-Baghdadi who gave me the orders!" said a now shaking and crying Kadyrov.

"The ISIS leader?"

"Yes! He told me to kill all of your family!"

"Why?"

"Because you always spoiled his plans," replied Kadyrov.

Chad, with all the strength and might he could gather, punched Kadyrov in the face, then a second and third time, before walking to the door, unlocking it, and calling the security person, who was walking back to the infirmary from his break. "Get the medical technician to attend to his injuries. He was biting his fingernails," said Chad before walking up to his office.

***

There was no investigation by the FBI as to how Kadyrov had lost three of his fingernails, with the fourth nail barely holding onto his digit. Kadyrov was transferred from the custody of the FBI to the US Marshals Service while the FBI drew up the charges against him. The FBI had thirty days to charge Kadyrov, but the Feds took less than one week to charge him with providing material support to ISIS and with the first-degree murder of the Knights. The murder and terrorism charges were filed in Federal District Court with the US Attorney for the District of Colorado in Denver. Kadyrov was indicted shortly thereafter on both charges.

After his indictment, Niko was found guilty after a jury trial and released on bond. The prosecution raised their objections in court to the release, but to no success. The federal judge, a retired army colonel and former JAG officer, rejected all of the prosecutor's objections. Chad himself didn't raise an objection to Niko's release. He looked rather happy that the terrorist Kadyrov was getting released. The court confiscated Niko's Canadian passport and also required him to wear an ankle monitor. Additionally, the court ordered Kadyrov to stay at a designated apartment complex until the sentencing date, set for two months later.

Three days after his release, Kadyrov committed suicide; he was found with the barrel and suppressor of a Remington model 1911 .45 caliber handgun in his mouth after blowing his brains out. The investigation by the Denver police revealed that the serial number on the weapon had been rasped off. How Kadyrov had acquired the weapon was the only unanswered question after the investigation was closed. The authorities ruled the death a suicide after no prints or forcible entry of the apartment were noted.

The Muslim terrorist from Uzbekistan and Chechnya with the Cheshire cat grin was dead.

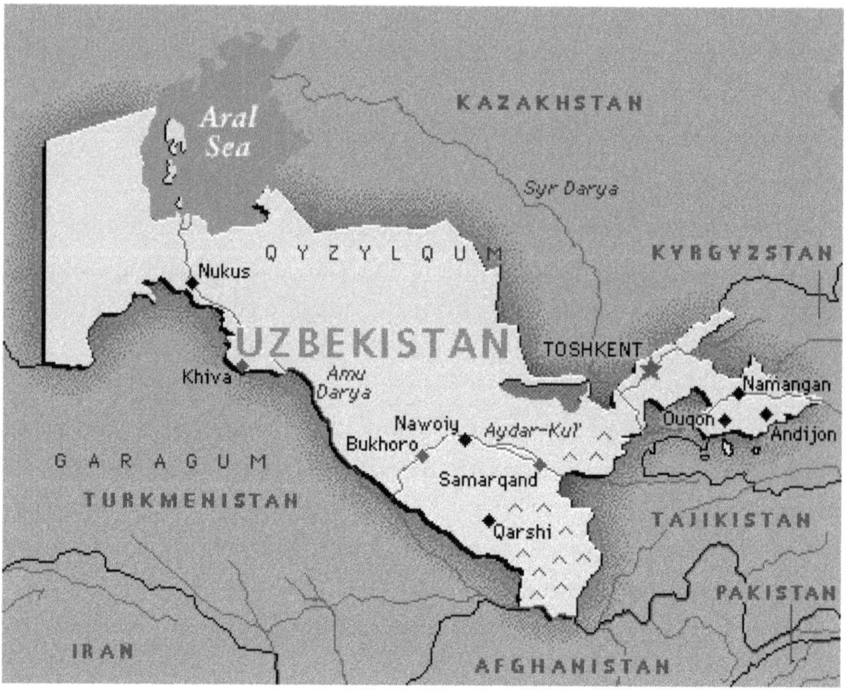
Aral Sea
KAZAKHSTAN
Syr Darya
QYZYLQUM
KYRGYZSTAN
Nukus
UZBEKISTAN
TOSHKENT
Khiva
Amu Darya
Namangan
Nawoiy
Aydar-Kul'
Quqon
Andijon
Bukhoro
GARAGUM
Samarqand
TURKMENISTAN
Qarshi
TAJIKISTAN
PAKISTAN
IRAN
AFGHANISTAN

Chapter 23

The stealth army helicopter from Joint Base Andrews landed at twelve midnight at Peterson AFB, approximately seventy-three miles south of Denver. Ten men, poisoned with deep grief and all appropriately dressed in black, were picked up by two black SUVs with tinted windows. No one said a word once they were in the SUVs, since each of them knew what their assignment was.

One hour later, they reached their destination in Denver; suddenly, all of the lights went out at the court-designated apartment complex where Kadyrov had been directed to reside by the judge. The apartment was located on 12th Avenue, off East Colfax Avenue. Niko was sound asleep but awoke when he felt being grabbed by the arms and legs by some very strong individuals. He was taken by complete surprise and was in total shock, unable to say anything for a moment. Was it the devil that had come to pay him a visit? Niko was sure the phantom men in black had silently come through the door without opening it. The room was pitch black and all the men were dressed in black. Niko could hardly make them out, although he could tell all were moving extremely fast. When the team trained for any mission, it was a marvel to see how fast each of these men could move, even though none had been hit by lightning like the Flash had. He could tell all of the men had night vision goggles because they had no problem moving around in the dark.

Niko struggled, to no avail, then felt cold iron rammed into his mouth. He tried to say no after he became aware it was the barrel of a gun, then he briefly saw a white light and heard a boom, both at exactly the same time. The next thing he saw was Mooney holding out her hand and saying, "Come with me, my darling." Niko felt his body fly away at that very moment.

His neighbors next door claimed they heard a minor struggle as soon as all the lights went out, a muffled sound, complete silence, and then a few moments later, the lights of the apartment complex came back on again. The neighbors heard no other noises.

The two black SUVs, parked in an alley behind the apartment complex, picked up the ten phantoms dressed in black and returned them back to the base. The stealth army helicopter left Peterson AFB at four in the morning, unnoticed by those not involved in the clandestine mission. CWO4 Padilla, team leader of the legendary Bravo Team, then made a call on a secured line. "Sir, the mission has been completed successfully," he said and hung up the phone without waiting for a response or feeling any remorse for what had just transpired.

***

As far as the FBI and Winters were concerned, the case on terrorist Niko Adel Kadyrov was closed. Winters got his revenge and was finally at peace. Now Winters had to deal with al-Baghdadi, who requested the mission, if the ISIS leader was still alive.

Chad knew that Raqqa had fallen recently after a heavy assault by Syrian Kurdish forces backed by the United States and other foreign fighters. Had al-Baghdadi been killed in that assault? Nobody had reported one way or the other, although there were rumors flying around that he was safe and sound after he was seen in a small village outside of Raqqa preaching his sermons of hate. Well, only time would tell. If al-Baghdadi was still alive, Winters would deal with him.

The Final Chapter

It had been a tiring sixty days for Chad. The federal terrorism and murder case against Niko Adel Kadyrov was "abated by death" by the US Attorney for the District of Colorado after Kadyrov was found dead. Chad felt exhausted, even though the trial had not taken long, but he was in a very joyous mood for a change. He felt like a heavy burden had been lifted off his shoulders now that the killer of the Knights was dead. He had been in his Washington, D.C., office for the past two weeks and was just getting back into the regular routine of his investigative work. He also felt good that his buddy, Tom Reynolds, was doing much better and might even regain partial use of his right arm. Everything was hunky dory as far as Chad was concerned. Life was good once again and he felt he was living it.

He left the office around seven that Friday evening, but not before he said his usual goodbyes to all of the employees working late. He got to his apartment and ate his usual ham and cheese sandwich for supper, which he bought at the neighborhood deli on his way home from work. After supper, Chad decided to listen to the CD the old retired sergeant major had given him during his last visit to the Knights' residence. Boy, that had been a long time ago. He sure missed them, especially his beloved Nora. She had been on his mind for the last couple of days. He turned the music on and was reclining in his easy chair when the CD got to Nora's favorite song. He had not heard the song since he'd first been told of the Knights' murder. Chad started feeling melancholy, tears rolling down his cheeks, and decided he had to get out of the old apartment and go for a walk or a drink. He had to get out in the open to clear his head.

A feeling Chad had never experienced before took over his body. He was not a drinker and hadn't had a beer in quite a long time, but now he felt like having one. He decided tonight was as good a time as any to start drinking, to see if he could get the funny feeling he was experiencing out of his system. He knew there was a neighborhood bar a couple of blocks away from his apartment and decided to walk there. It wasn't a good idea to drive if he was going to drink.

He was about one block away from the bar when he saw the beautiful slender woman in the tight blue dress across the street. He froze. That funny feeling in his body became even stronger. Then, all of a sudden, he felt euphoria take over his entire body. His memory flashed back to the first day he had met Nora, when they'd played golf together. He remembered that she had said, after the golf game, "Leave a little bit of sparkle wherever you go, Chad."

"It can't be, but it's her! Nora! Nora!" he yelled as he excitedly ran across the street to catch up with the beautiful lady in blue. Chad never saw the furniture delivery truck barreling down the street. At last, he was reunited with the beautiful Nora Knight, the love of his life, now and forever. Rest in peace, FBI Special Agent Chadwick Winters. Rest in peace.

Lightning Source UK Ltd.
Milton Keynes UK
UKHW041856071118
331957UK00003B/47/P

9 781525 527487